To Pav,

DARKEST
LIGHT

Hope you enjoy it.

Alex

A special thank you goes to Artist
Fyodor Ananiev, for designing the book
cover and other artwork he is creating.

DARKEST LIGHT

ALEX TAYLOR

To order additional copies of this book, contact:
Xlibris
800-056-3182
www.Xlibrispublishing.co.uk
Orders@Xlibrispublishing.co.uk
650881

Contents

Preface and Acknowledgments

I would like to introduce you to my deep thoughts – an imaginary story, a story that has kept me busy for the past fifteen months. I take this opportunity to thank you for embarking on the journey through *Darkest Light*. Writing while studying and working hasn't been easy, but in the end, I succeeded – because I kept positive and never gave up.

All my friends and my family have supported me and helped me stay motivated. Through tough times, they offered valuable feedback and listening ears as I shared endless hours of ideas. I offer a special thank you to all my social network friends who commented on or liked my posts and updates. You made this book happen. Without your ongoing support, this book would not be as it is today. You are friends for life.

Darkest Light's main character is Michael. Get to know him; he is not so bad. I made him a loving, peaceful guy. His journey will keep you intrigued, and hopefully, his love story will touch your hearts.

Keep safe and never give up on your dreams, no matter how far away they might seem.

Lots of love,

Alex xx

CHAPTER 1

Dark

Bzz, bzz, bzzz, bzzz.

The alarm wakes me with a sudden fright. Barely opening my eyes, I look at the alarm clock. Seeing it's not even 6.00 a.m. yet, I roll onto my side and close my eyes, which feel heavy. I can hardly move, as I'm pinned down by my thick quilt – very comfortable, all tucked in, warm. I can hear the fizzing sound of the thunder, and the room lights up for a split second as lightning strikes. There's an unrelenting sound of rain as it hits the pavement hard. The raindrops against the window and make a loud ticking sound. I feel a cool slight breeze on my face because the window is slightly open.

Bzz, bzz, bzzz, bzzz.

The alarm is still going off, and the cool air discourages me from getting out of bed. Sleepily, I bash the alarm button to silence it. I unfold the quilt over me and slowly sit upright. *Do I really want to go to work today? Surely I can call in and say I am not feeling very well. But what if I lose my job over it? Is it really worth it?*

I stand up, dazed, and stumble across the room to shut the window, a very old window with its green paint peeled off. The glass is dirty, and a crack goes through one of the panels. Placing my hands on each corner of the window, I push down with all my strength. Not even a slight shift. It doesn't seem to want to close, as the wood is swollen due to getting wet over time. I have no choice but to leave it as it is. Water spits inside as it hits the ledge. I feel the damp carpet beneath my naked feet.

I gaze into the distance and notice how gloomy the day is going to be. The sky is covered in thick dark clouds; the street lights are still on. I'm not really a morning person. In fact, I hate getting up early.

'Brr, it's blistering cold in 'ere.'

I do not usually mind the rain and thunderstorms. In fact, I love feeling cosy in the warmth of my bed, although my double bed feels empty; I miss the warmth of a woman next to me. Disoriented, I stumble back across the room and lie in my bed once again. I pull the quilt up to my neck to get warmed up. Lying on my side, I stare at the alarm clock as it flickers through different times; I reach down and unplug it.

'What the hell?'

The alarm clock still flickers through different times …7.35 down to 6.24 a.m. I bash it with my fist a couple of times, which does not make a difference. This urges me to get out of bed and fix it. But I feel way too cosy to get out of bed just yet. It's way too early.

I start deliberating …pondering … not thinking straight, as I definitely had too much to drink last night. What was I thinking of going out alone, drinking all those pints? I rub my forehead, pressing hard on the right side of my temple. I feel drained and have that hangover sick feeling. My head is pounding like I have been hit with a brick several times.

I finally decide to get out of bed. I sit upright on the side and reach over to the top drawer of my bedside cabinet. I pull it open, grabbing a fresh packet of cigarettes and my toolkit. Nothing like a cigarette to start the day. I know they are bad for my health, but that does not stop me from opening the packet and sliding a cigarette out. Lighting it and taking a deep breath of smoke seems to make things worse, by the way I'm feeling.

Again I ponder the purpose of my life. I presume about ten minutes go by. I decide to stand up. I feel rather dizzy, so I sit back down and relax for a while. I shut my eyes.

A few minutes pass, and my intense curiosity urges me to try to fix the alarm clock. I remove the screws from the bottom of the device and stare inside. Nothing seems wrong. All the wires are still attached. I tap the inside of it with the screwdriver and play with it for a while. Nothing, still the same problem. I place it back on the bedside cabinet opened and start getting ready for work.

I lumber across the room in just a T-shirt and underwear. I pull open the wardrobe door, take out my only suit, and put it on my bed. I pull out a shirt and a tie, and I grab some underwear from the second drawer of my bedside cabinet. I walk out of the bedroom and stagger across the hall. I press my hand against the wall as I drag myself along the hallway. I switch on the light and pull the cord to start the shower to warm it up. I slide the shower curtain across to avoid water flooding the bathroom floor. I walk to the sink and splash my face with cold water, as I still feel quite queasy. Putting a hand on each side of the sink, I pull my head down for a while. *Today is going to be a really tough day for me. Why am I feeling so down?*

'Pull yourself together, Michael,' I say out loud. No one can hear me anyway. I need to get on with it and shower. Surely that will make me feel better, and it will definitely wake me up.

I pull my T-shirt over my head and remove my boxers, leaving them on the floor near the sink base. Slowly but surely I get into the shower. As I stand in the shower, I just can't stop thinking about this woman I have never met, waiting for me in the bedroom, waiting for my attention, for me to kiss her slowly and hold her tightly in my arms as we snooze in bed before getting up for breakfast. Anyone can dream, right?

All these daydreams … passing time. Have to get out of the shower. Still have to eat breakfast and get dressed. I need to snap out of the way I'm feeling. I grasp onto the towel hanging on the rail and dry myself as quickly as possible. The slight breeze hits my wet skin and gives me goosebumps all over. My whole body vibrates as I shiver. I wrap the towel around my waist and walk back into the bedroom, where I get dressed. As I button my shirt, I notice the time on the alarm clock reads 5.30 a.m. That starts to freak me out because I can't imagine why the clock would be behaving like this. I have to ignore the device. Something seems to be playing on my mind, but I definitely have no time for jokes today.

'Ah, what a day!'

Showering does not really help how I'm feeling, but at least I smell really good. I spray on some aftershave and head downstairs. The old wooden staircase creeks as I make my way down. I rush, as time is ticking.

Once downstairs, I open the fridge, realizing all I have are bread and a box of eggs. So I make myself eggs on toast for breakfast. I sit down at the table and eat. Breakfast does make me feel somewhat better, but my curiosity still keeps me thinking about how to solve the problem with the alarm clock.

Before I walk out of the front door, I put my lunch in the briefcase, sit down at the table, and smoke one last cigarette. As I get to the end of the cigarette, I reach into my briefcase and wear the watch I usually keep in there. I gaze at it for a few seconds. It says 5.30. 'What is going on?' Having no idea what time it is makes me feel slightly anxious and frustrated. This just does not make any sense at all.

I grab my keys, wallet, cigarettes, lighter, and briefcase and open the front door. Torrential rain smashes onto the ground, soaking everything in its path. I take an umbrella, as I cannot afford to get my suit wet. I shut the door behind me and start walking up the road. No one else seems to be out, just me and a couple of stray cats hiding under parked cars.

As I walk, my surroundings start to change. I look behind me, and everything is just black. Everything has disappeared …no cars, no road and no doors. The sky is completely black, and I cannot see any stars or the moon. Things have changed very rapidly. It's not even raining anymore, so I close the umbrella. I cannot hear a sound; it's as if I am in a vacuum. I'm on a dark, secluded, black path, but in the distance, I see a small light on the side, where doors used to be before. I walk a few paces forward. Nothing is happening. The mysterious light illuminates the path ahead of me, and it seems alluring.

'Hello! Hello! What the hell is going on here?' I shout. But nothing. Not even an echo. And I can barely hear my own voice, no matter how loudly I shout.

I can't seem to move. 'Why did I not just stay in bed?' I ask myself softly. I am very afraid, but at the same time, I am eager to know what is going on. I seem to be frozen on the spot, as I am very cautious of my new, unsettling surroundings. I light up a cigarette to relieve my nerves.

CHAPTER 2

Nervous

I stand still, feeling the nerves go through me like impulses. Panic. Is that really the word though? Does *panic* explain my situation? I'm all alone. I can't hear anything. Nothing is happening ... *Why is this happening to me? Am I freaking out? I think so.*

What is this? I cannot explain what's really on my mind. Even the cats have disappeared.

I'm anxious but intrigued at the same time. My body is frozen solid, and I'm unsure of what I should do next. 'What is going on?' I mutter, pretty sure no one is listening. I take a pace forward, very cautious and not in a rush at this point.

My heart beats hard as my nerves elevate.

I hesitate to keep moving. 'I cannot go any farther.' I whisper. I am not sure what lies ahead.

Once again, I light up a cigarette, but this time I sit down. I'm not really sure why. I guess I just want to get myself back together. I'm in shock. I just sit here, silent. I take a deep breath in, feeling my thoracic region inflate as air pours down my trachea. I'm starting to relax a little, and my thoughts start running wild.

Someone unknown to me, someone that appears in my mind. I keep thinking about this woman, though I've never laid my eyes on her. Still, I imagine long black hair. It shines and shimmers, looking soft and clean. Her eyes are hazel with a small hint of dark green. I'm looking closely at them, and I see a few tiny specs of yellow. Every time she looks into my eyes, a dagger pierces my heart sharply. I can't resist temptation; so much magnetism hangs in the air. Her skin, sleek and silky, feels warm against my fingertips, which slide down her face and then gently down the side of her neck. I grab her arm and pull her toward me. Her lips are tender and have a delicate look about them. This girl has imperfections, but they make her even more perfect for me, adding to her divine beauty. Her body; just perfect. She's so enticing, but I know I'm only daydreaming again. Why would she want me? I cannot take her anywhere. I'm stuck in blackness. If only she were by my side and we were approaching the light together. I would give her a part of me.

Her supple lips are getting closer to mine.

I should start moving towards that light. I have been sitting here for a while now. I still can't tell what time it is, as my watch doesn't even have a face anymore. The glass is completely black. I get in an upright position and start walking. The glow is getting brighter and bigger. I'm still quite nervous, but at the same time, I am feeling relaxed as though I'm without a care in the world. Nothing makes sense here. My pace is steady, and my thoughts are focused only on her. Each and every detail about her feels like a breath of fresh air, a morning breeze. But she isn't present. I can't perform miracles, but I still keep a smirk on my face. The thing is I'm still in the same situation as I was two minutes ago. Nothing has changed, except that I'm a little bit closer to the light.

The farther I walk, the brighter the light gets. But I'm getting really tired of walking. That sheer boredom of walking on my own in complete emptiness. I wish I could just get there now and see what lies beyond.

I start daydreaming once again. All my life, I have always been so nice to everyone; I've never hated anyone. I'm always helping people around me, and it seems that life kicks you in your behind when you are kind and always there for people. Maybe this phenomenon is a sign that I should change who I am. *But why should I?* Why should I be at their level – treating people like garbage, cheating on partners, and not appreciating what earth has to offer? I know I am not always right, but I know that respecting others as much as I respect myself is not a lousy trait to have. On the other hand, should I treat others like gold, if I don't get the same treatment?

I remember those days when my parents used to struggle to feed me, but they always succeeded, always fed me before feeding themselves. Why can I not be like other people? Born and raised in a comfortable life, given most things I desire? It's not that simple. I have worked hard all my life, and I've always learnt that respect is something you have to earn. I do miss my parents dearly. I think of the birthdays they've missed and those all-important days as a family. 'I wish I could see you both again'

'What is the purpose of thinking these thoughts?'

I feel so wise. Yet I am walking all alone in this darkness, with no one to talk to, talking to myself.

The more I think, the more life seems to make sense to me. But still, it feels as if nothing matters; my worthless existence is not going to change for the better if I don't help myself. I'm in a deep hole trying to work as hard as I can to get out, but whatever I seem to do, nothing seems to work in my favour. As for my job, I have been working hard for years with the same company, and I'm still on the same salary as I was when I started. I see a lot of people come into the company and then get promotions and better opportunities. Where is my opportunity? Where is my happy ending to this life full of misfortunates? 'Michael, stop complaining and get on with it.' I say to myself.

'I feel so crazy right now …so empty.'

Wow, I am talking to myself.

For once, I can scream and shout and act like an idiot, with no one to judge me.

At least I don't feel hung-over anymore! Eggs on toast did the trick.

'Ahhhhhhhhhhhhhhhhhhhhhhhhhhhhhhhhhhhhhhhhhhhh,' I shout, but not even an echo comes back to me.

I open my briefcase and grab the drink I packed before I came out. I unscrew the top and sip it slowly. The liquid hits the back of my throat, quenching my thirst. I do not finish it off, as I cannot be sure what lies ahead.

The glow of the light hits my face. It can't be that far now. I could easily run to the source of the light; it can't be more than a hundred metres away from me. But running in my suit wouldn't be such a good idea, and I don't want to over exert myself. I switch off my thoughts and decide to go with the flow. I start running.

'Damn!' I shout. Today's definitely not going to be my day. The catch on the lock of my briefcase has released, and its innards have scattered all over the place. I feel frustrated; I had a lot of paperwork, and it's spread out everywhere.

As I pick up my scattered papers, stacking them neatly, I notice a piece of hard coloured, thin cardboard. I notice what looks like a handwritten note, and it's definitely not my writing. I've never seen this notecard before.

It just says, 'Beyond the light, be prepared for the unknown.'

How strange! *How am I supposed to prepare myself for the unknown?* I ignore the note and place all the paperwork back in my briefcase, picking the rest of the stuff that dropped. I lock my briefcase back up. I notice that my shoelace is untied, so I tie it back up and start walking. Not long until I get there.

I walk slowly and think.

For the first time today, I feel positive. I'm not sure why! But I have a feeling that, beyond that light, my dreams will come true. Problem is, I am not sure what my dreams are.

What are your dreams? Find a partner, have children, a good career, live in a comfortable home? What is the purpose of you living on such a beautiful earth? Why do you not set yourself a goal in life and follow it through, every step of the way. Give yourself that chance, because in the world we live in, no one will give you that chance; only you can make an opportunity work for you. Hesitation is something that stops most people from believing in themselves and following their dreams. Today is the day to change. Why tomorrow?

For me, today's phenomenon has really put life into perspective. But at the same time, I am very confused as to what is happening. I definitely can't clarify my thoughts, and this circumstance has never arisen before.

I look ahead. The white light is just a few steps away. I hold my hand out in front of my face, and I keep trying to look away. But the glow is so alluring, and I cannot help being enticed by it.

I wonder what is going to happen. Nothing lies beyond. Just a black empty space.

I walk close and stand in front of the light. I am now facing it, head on. It looks a little bit bigger than a large door. Though it's so bright it's hard to look at, it is seductive. I squint from the pain. I hesitate to touch it as I have no clue what will happen once I make contact with it.

'Helllooo? Helllloooo.' Nothing. Not even an echo comes back, and only total silence reaches my ears. Even my voice has become totally muted.

CHAPTER 3

Beyond the Light

Before I step into the unknown, I light up a cigarette to calm myself. By now, I've started sweating. I play with my tie, loosening it. I start deliberating and speculating as to what will happen once I walk through this luminous bright light.

'Am I dead?' I wonder.

Nah, I can't be, I think. 'I mean, I'm talking to myself.'

I flick the three-quarters of the lit cigarette away from me, and slowly, I start pacing towards the light. I reach out as far as I can with my right hand. I cannot feel anything, but I am getting vacuumed by the light; slowly, my whole body seems to be getting swallowed. It feels like I'm in a trance. And from this moment, I can't stop myself from what I am experiencing.

I try to hold back from being pulled in by the light 'What ammmm I dooinnnnggggg?' I kneel down, and I try to grasp onto the hard ground. It's no use. I'm slowly getting sucked in.

Then, as if the light never existed, I'm in the unknown.

I look behind me, and the light has completely disappeared. All I can see is a vast desert. It looks desolate, with a few dead trees and a small lake. The water appears black as tar and calm; in fact, it's completely still, like it's made of black ice. A slight breeze blows the sand around.

What is this place?

I look to my front and to my sides.

'Wow, what a view,' I've never seen anything like this before.

I see trees that I have never seen in my life – large trunks, bluish purple leaves, some bearing fruit that doesn't even exist.

The grass here is a turquoise colour. I sit down and feel the ground beneath me. I brush my palms over the turquoise meadow, and the grass feels velvety against the surface of my hand. Tiny red flowers with purple-tipped petals bloom from what seems to be rich soil.

I inhale a deep breath in. 'Ahhh that's nice.' The air feels so fresh; my airways are clearing as I breathe in. The slight chilled breeze brushes against my face, making me feel refreshed. The sky looks like a sunset sky, but the sun is not setting. This sun looks much bigger than ours, and it's a reddish colour. I don't feel any gravitational change at all.

Gazing around me, I ask, 'Am I on a different planet?'

I have no idea what to expect. I hesitate to stand up and start walking, but sheer curiosity forces me to start exploring. If the foliage is different from what I'm used to, then I can't be sure of what animals live here.

I stand up. 'Right ... Time to move on and start examining my new surroundings.'

I walk to the nearest tree. I stroke the bark. 'That's nice.' It feels like the skin of a kiwi. 'Very interesting.' I use my key to scratch the bark. As I scratch hard, a secretion starts oozing out from the scratch; it's dark blue and smells quite bad. Its consistency is similar to a thick hair gel. The tree bears some kind of fruit, like rugby balls but much smaller, with rubbery spikes coming out of their skin. On the top, the fruit is held by a stem attached to the branch.

I cut one down and start hacking at it with the key ... 'Woahh.' I drop the fruit as it insanely opens up and a creature darts out and flies off.

'What was that?' Only the open fruit of the skin, spread out on the turquoise grass, remains.

I cut another one of these pods and save it for later. Maybe I could try to capture the creature and examine it further.

The tree itself smells rather fruity, but where is this sweet aroma coming from? Despite the awful smell of the secretion oozing out of the scratched bark, the fruity smell still overcomes it. I instantly grab a leaf and nibble at it, expecting it to taste like the leaves I'm used to.

'Wow, this tastes amazing.'

The leaf is very sweet, yet has a sour aftertaste that is quite nice. In the distance, there seem to be hundreds of these trees, so I don't bother to collect leaves but move on.

Walking down the hill towards what seems to be a nice pleasant walking path, I notice some red bushes that remind me of autumn leaves. Insects swarm around them, no doubt attracted to the aroma of nectar the bushes give off. I can't be sure what kind of insects they are, so I just ignore them and keep moving. I look around me and see only trees of the same sort and these weird-looking bushes.

After a few minutes of walking, I notice some rocks on the side of the path. I move closer to them. Bright green and around a metre in length, three of them stand alone in a row. As I inspect them, I notice that one of these rocks has a wide crack across the top of it. I look inside the crack, and it seems some kind of glass texture coating fills the rock. I try to open up the crack to enable further investigation, but even hitting it with a pebble doesn't do anything. Could it be a huge diamond inside with a layer of rock to camouflage its precious content? I place both hands on the front of the rock and push with all my might. But it's too heavy. Nothing happens; the rock won't budge.

As I continue my investigation, it occurs to me that I can discern no purpose for my visit to this world. *Why am I here?*

'I'm being tested. Back home the sun rises in the east and sets in the west.' Here the sun is not moving at all. But there must be an explanation. I need to give it more time.

In front of me, this path stretches out far into the distance, and I can see a split at the end. Alongside the path are the trees with edible leaves and fruit that bear creatures inside them, bushes of different colours and weird-looking insects hovering around them, and the odd boulder here and there. I decide to go off the path and start walking on the grass, through this world's vast forest.

I refrain from moving quickly, as I'm unaware of what lies ahead of me. I don't want to get lost. But why does that matter? I am lost.

I look at my broken watch. 'I wonder what time it is.'

I walk through the forest, and soon, I notice some really strange things. The same trees are plentiful here, and many different coloured bushes sit in clusters in every direction I look. The bark on some of the trees seems to be pulsating. Surely the trees are not living creatures. For the moment, I dare to go near them, not sure what to expect. I keep my distance as I move cautiously through the forest. My heartbeat is quite elevated, and I'm sweating.

Looking into the distance, I notice a small opening in this vast forest that seems to be an open field. As I walk, I gaze at the sky; no clouds block my vision of the sun. It's easy to look at without hurting my eyes, as it's not as bright as our sun. I can also see four distinct moons. Small meteorites glow, as they hit the atmosphere and burn up, leaving a trail of light behind them. *Amazing.*

I pace forward gradually, trying to be as quiet as I can. But I step on dead branches and leaves, and I'm making quite a racket. The branches snap, and the dry leaves rustle as they get crushed under my feet. I am still looking up.

I start hearing weird noises in the distance – squawking sounds that suggest a flock of birds. But I can't see anything yet.

So far, nothing much has happened here. I have to admit, as weird as this place seems, it is quite an amazing, peaceful place. I still haven't encountered a hint of darkness, as the sun sits high up in the sky. The physics of this place don't make any sense at all. If our sun was as close to our earth, everything would burn away, all the water would evaporate, and nothing would be able to survive. Yet here, everything seems to be flourishing.

As I get closer to the open field, I notice a flock of some kind of flying creatures.

'*Wow*! What beauties!' I shout too loudly.

I crouch down so I can't be seen. At the end of the day, I don't want to draw attention to myself; after all, I might be attacked.

There must be at least twenty of the massive, colourful creatures. Their bellies are bright yellow, and the large feathers on their wings are a purple pattern with red at each tip. And at the end of each feather, I see what seems to be a light blue glow; as they fly past me, they leave a trail of light behind.

How weird. I can't make out the faces as they are flying quite rapidly, but all I can say is that these creatures look majestic.

I wait until they are no longer in my view and slowly raise myself from the crouching position, tucking my shirt back in as I get up. I start pacing forward again. I grasp onto my briefcase.

Walking stealthily, I nearly step on what appears to be a snake-like creature. Its skin seems to be peeling, and it is motionless. It has no limbs and, apparently, no eyelids. It just sits there on the grass, doing absolutely nothing. Not sure if it's dangerous or aggressive, I move closer to it to examine it further. The creature opens its mouth wide, as if yawning. It has no teeth at all, and its tongue is light green. Even though its shedding its skin, it looks very colourful, though the colours are dull. Without hesitation, I place my right hand on its head to feel the skin. Other than the flaky peel, it seems to have a nice smooth texture to it. I grab the creature in my hands and stroke its head.

It's purring like a cat. How strange.

Suddenly, I hear screams coming from up ahead. Could this be? Another human here? I run towards the gap in the trees, clutching my briefcase in between my body and my right arm and holding the creature on my shoulder with my left palm so I won't drop it.

The screams get louder and louder and clearer. It is definitely a guy screaming for help.

As I close in on the gap, I slow down. I do not want to attract any unwanted attention, and I need to assess what is going on before I try to attempt to save the man who is clearly in need of help.

CHAPTER 4

I get to the opening. On either side of me are two of the trees I first encountered. I crouch down. Ahead is one of the huge flying creatures. I see that its wingspan is massive. The creature seems angry, and the guy in front of it is on the ground, fending it off with his backpack. He stands no chance, and I need to help him get out of there.

Holding tightly to my briefcase, I throw it with all my might, hitting the creature in the face. It looks at me, hisses, and flies off into the distance.

'I'm coming. Stay there,' I call out. 'I mean you no harm.'

I need to get this man back here where it seems to be safe and where none of the creatures can get to. The gaps in between the trees are good to keep us safe for a while. The man holds his arm up as he notices me.

'Hey, I'm Michael. Can you walk?'

In a rusty voice, he answers, 'Michael, my name is Rickard. My legs seem to be paralysed. I can't feel anything. I took a pretty bad hit.'

'Okay, Rick, I am going to move you to a safer place. I won't be able to carry you. You're twice my size.'

'G-grab both my arms and drag me,' he stutters. 'Cheers, Michael.'

He seems to be in bad shape; his face is very sweaty and off colour. I grab both his arms and drag him into the wooded area without hesitation.

I sit down on the grass and hold his back upright.

'Michael.'

'Rick, stay with me. I'm still here.'

'I can still see and feel you, Mike. Can I call you Mike?'

'Yes of course. Please do. Can you tell me how you got here?'

'Yessss. Mike ... I'm sorry if I lose you now and agaaiiinnnn. Not going to last long like this.'

I feel really sorry for him. He can barely keep his eyes open. He pauses for a few minutes. I check his pulse to make sure he is alive. His pulse feels very weak, but it's still going, and he is still breathing.

'Mike?'

'Yes, Rick. I'm still here, buddy.'

'Mike?'

'I'm here.'

'Thank you for helping me out back there.' He groans.

'I'm sorry I can't do anymore, mate. I really wish I could heal you somehow; you don't look so well.'

'Hey ... I was walking home, right after I'd done my food shopping. And I passed out, somehow ... I can't remember. All I remember was that it was quite a dull day.' He coughs unintentionally.

I rub his back.

'I think I passed out, but I can't remember how, to be perfectly honest. Let me tell you something about myself ... It would be a shame to die a complete stranger to you.'

He starts coughing again, this time uncontrollably, and I push him slightly forward to help him clear his airway.

'My full name is Rickard Shane Ashmore. I was originally born in a small village in the northern parts of London. My dad was English, and my mother came from a town called Brattleboro in Vermont, USA. I was quite young and do not remember it much, but my mum used to tell me about it.' He takes a deep breath. 'So many trees, she used to say, of all different colours – red, orange, green. She'd tell me all about the lake, fishing trips with Dad, and our little cottage near the woods. My father met her when he was quite young on a school trip. They stayed friends and got closer and closer, writing each other letters.' He smiles. 'Eventually my mum moved to be near Dad, and they had me. Soon after, we ended up living in Brattleboro. I do remember some good memories, but we moved back to England when I was only seven, so most of my childhood was in North London.'

He pauses for quite a long time.

'Rick?'

'Sooooo sorrryyy, Mike. I cannot go on any longer. I feel faint and like I'll black out any moment now.'

'Relax. Take it easy. You don't have to continue, but your story is soothing to my ears. Take your time. I would love to hear more, mate.'

He looks at me with his eyes half open and grins. Then he coughs loudly.

'Nice to see you smile in this situation, mate. I have been wandering around this place for a while, and I can't be sure what to make of it. I'm supposed to be at work, but instead I'm here.'

'Yeah? I was looking forward to having my usual tuna salad for lunch. Ahhhhhh …'

'Rick? Are you okay?'

'Just a sharp pain on the right side of my abdomen. It's gone now, but I'm drained. You know, I met this woman at my local supermarket, and our meeting was a complete accident. She picked up a can of peas and dropped it, and the can rolled and hit my foot. I remember her running towards me and apologizing as I was picking it up. We became best friends and eventually lovers. We were together for three years, and a year ago, she left me for another man.'

'Wow, so sorry to hear that, mate.'

'Nah, my fault. I became a recluse, always wanted to be on my own. Forgot how special she was and how much I loved her till she left me. Don't make the same mistake as I did, Mike.'

I can tell he's really hanging in there; as he talks, his voice is getting rustier and rustier.

'Cheers, mate, really appreciate your advice, although I have no one in my life, just dreams of a woman.'

'Make those dreams come true … Listen, make sure you take my lucky backpack when I die. Keep it safe; there might be something in it you can use. I have had it for many years, I class it as lucky because my granddad gave it to me.' He coughs. 'I don't think I am going to last much…'

'*Rick*?! Are you still with me, bud?'

He coughs again.

I feel a little panicked, and I'm not sure what to do to help him. He looks so pale, and his body rests on my arm like a cloth. He isn't moving much, and his breathing is hardly noticeable. I place two fingers on his neck. His pulse rate is very slow.

'What can I do to help you?'

'Miii ...'

'Stay with me. Don't close your eyes. I'm still here.'

I can't leave him like this; I could do with a companion here. He is a well-built man, much bigger in stature then me, yet he is so weak and helpless right now. He grasps my wrist gently, using the last bit of strength in his body.

'Miiike,' he says, drawing the word out and gasping for breath before continuing. 'Please ...'

'Rick, I'm here. Yes? What can I do for you, mate?'

'Please, leave me here to die,' he pants.

I cannot listen to him; I can't just leave him here on his own. I gently lay him down on the ground and start gathering leaves, bits of moss, and soft bits of turf to make him a pillow. I push the small pile near his body. I lift his head and place all the gathered bits underneath before gently lowering his head onto the pile.

He slowly raises his arm. 'Thank you, Mike. It was an honour to meet you today. Thank you for your help.'

'Rick, I certainly enjoyed talking to you. You seem like such a nice guy. It's a shame we couldn't have explored this place together.'

I wait for a moment, hoping to hear him one more time, but only silence hangs between us.

'Still with me, Rick?'

He doesn't respond. No thoughts run through my head; I just feel very sad.

I place two fingers on his wrist. Nothing. I kneel near his body, hold his left hand, and bow my head in silence for a while. Then I place his right hand on his body and his left hand on his right hand. I walk around the vicinity for a while, hoping to gather a bunch of flowers. Not much is here in terms of flowers, but I do find some great-looking leaves of all different colours, which I cut down and arrange in a bunch. I place them on his chest.

'Rest in peace, Rickard Shane Ashmore. May your soul find serenity.'

I feel so sorry for this guy. I didn't know him well enough to cry, but I do feel really sad about his death, not to mention losing the only link to the human world I'd found in this strange place. Rick seemed like a good guy with a good routine who'd been through a lot, from what he told me. I mean, wow, he lived in Brattleboro when he was a child. I remember having looked at pictures of the town, as it isn't too far from New York City. Such a green place, I recall; the air is probably fresh all year round and it seems like a good place to relax.

I grab Rick's backpack and drag it close to me, not opening it out of respect. It doesn't feel heavy at all and I'll easily be able to carry it on my back. I never asked Rick his age, but he looked to be in his mid-forties, a mature man. He deserves the utmost respect.

I sit down on the grass near him, feeling dreadful. He seemed to die happy, and my company helped him I think. I could search his pockets to check for identification and such, but I don't wish to disturb his dead corpse.

I run out to the open field to get my briefcase back, leaving the backpack near Rick's body, as I'm not leaving the area just yet. The briefcase is open, and everything seems to have disappeared from inside it. *I know I threw it at the creature, but everything's gone!* I don't understand. When I pick up the empty briefcase, I notice a note that reads, 'She will be near.'

Again this note doesn't make sense. I leave the briefcase where it lies, as I can't use it. I notice the fruit I picked up earlier from the tree. But it's open, and the creature has obviously flown off. I've seen plenty of the trees, and I shouldn't have a problem finding another to investigate.

I walk back to Rick and sit down near his head, just to pay my respects. I feel it would be rude to just leave straightaway. The creature I found earlier is still here. It doesn't move much, although it seems to be transforming into something. As its skin peels, it's developing limbs and its colour is brightening up a bit also. Since I found Rick, it has formed small teeth in its upper jaw, and a beautiful dark blue crest has formed along its spine.

CHAPTER 5

Attacked

Eventually, I leave Rick behind; I can't stay there much longer. I'm now carrying his backpack on my back, and though I'm still in my suit, I'm looking rather scruffy, with my shirt untucked and my tie loose. Also, my trousers are grass-stained, only the stain is turquoise instead of green. I gently pick up my creature and start walking back to the path I originally came from. Along the way, I pick a few of the leaves from the trees and eat them, wondering why they taste so good.

Looking up, I observe that the sun's position hasn't changed, but a fifth moon has appeared from behind the sun. It's probably the same size as our moon but seems to be green with what look like oceans. Am I looking at earth? It looks very similar. Maybe there is life on that moon also. The other moons look more like our moon, but three of them are nearly double its size, and the other one seems to be much smaller. I wonder how they affect the tides here.

I'm not far from the path now. The creature's limbs seem to have gotten bigger. I figure it may be able to start walking soon. I stop and place it on the floor. The creature stretches out, and as it's doing so, a tail forms and its limbs seem to be getting even longer. The skin all over its body is shedding, and the creature has now formed eyelids to protect its fully developed cornea. The colouration has changed to a dark red with yellow clover-like spots all over its body, and the crest on its back is a dark blue with a slight purple at the bottom. Looking closely at its feet, I see that the creature has four toes and, at the end of each, a formidable claw. The creature's skin is quite bumpy all over its back and sides, but the crest is smooth. Three longish curvy horns on either side of its face have developed, and its complexion is quite scaly looking. Its eyes, on either side of its head, are bright green.

This transformation makes me feel very wary, as my companion now seems dangerous. I leave it there and start moving quickly, walking as swiftly as I can to get as far from it as possible. I cannot risk dying without knowing why I'm here.

I look back, and in the distance, the creature is running towards me. I start running as fast as I can.

The creature chases me. Up ahead is the path, where I turn a sharp left and keep running. Going downhill now, I'm running faster and faster.

I trip over a couple of stones on the path 'Ouchhhh,' I shout as I tumble down hard. My body slams to the ground. I'm lying face down on the hard landscape, feeling pain in both my knees. And my face feels like it's been pelted with stones. Feeling a tear run down my face, I push myself up with both my arms and get up as quickly as I can. I resume running again but know I can't keep this up for long. So I stop. I seem to have hurt my legs quite badly. Moving away again, this time at a fast limp, I look back. And the creature is right behind me.

It's not doing anything. It's just standing there on all fours, wagging its tail as if it was a dog. I get closer to the creature and pat it. It starts purring and shutting its eyelids as I'm petting its head.

'Hey, little dude.'

Prrrrrrrrrprrrrrrrrr.

It seems like I've made a new friend and am no longer alone. I'm not sure what to feed it or how to take care of it. I've never had a pet in my life – nothing like this anyway. Such a sweet little creature. Its tail is quite long, and it's quite short and stumpy. It's not aggressive in the slightest and seems to like me. I'm not really sure why. Surely its kind has never seen a human before.

Looking down at my trousers, I see I've torn them at the knees. I stroke my face and discover that I have a cut too and it's bleeding. I rub the wound gently with my sleeve to clean the blood from my face. I'm still bleeding slightly, but the cut doesn't seem serious. I limp towards a tree a few steps away from me, grab a leaf, and use it to try to stop the bleeding. I tear the leaf in half and place it over the cut; it seems to be working. My legs still ache, so I decide to sit down for a while. I can't be limping everywhere. I should have just trusted the creature and waited for its metamorphosis to be complete. I can be very patient most times, but I kind of panicked and had to leave the area.

I place the backpack near me, as it's just extra weight on my back. And I start relaxing. The creature comes close and lies near my legs, allowing me to stroke its head.

'How sweet.' I say out loud. *I need to find a way to get this creature to come back to my world with me.*

That would be so awesome; I imagine waking up in the morning with this creature on my bed asleep. My friends would be impressed anyway.

I think of all the kids I've known and their first pets – how much attention they gave those little critters and how proud they were of their new friends.

I rub my grazed knees. They still hurt, and the injury feels more like a burn than anything else.

In front of me along the path is a row of bushes like hedges, and behind them, I see only trees, all the same kind. Suddenly, I notice rustling sounds. 'What is that?' I whisper to my creature.

I slowly push myself back with my legs so I'm no longer on the path but, rather, sitting on the grass.

The rustling continues, and my creature is now facing the bushes, hissing loudly.

'Come here, boy!'

Hsssssssssssss. Sssssssss. Hsssssssssssssssssssss.

Feeling a sudden panic, as I'm not sure what is going to happen, I stand up and start moving backwards. I'm not sure what to expect or what to do next. A tree obstructs my way, so I clutch it, pressing myself against it – fearing for my life.

Three creatures jump out of the bushes, staring at me. They look like wolves wildly growling. The wild beast senses my fear. My creature hisses wildly – a sound that's like nothing I've ever heard before.

The bodies of these wolfish beasts look very dangerous. Their bodies are completely black and hairless. Their rough skin resembles the bulging dry skin of a toad, and tiny tentacles protrude from their backs. They have yellow eyes with black oval-shaped pupils, large fangs, and very long tails that end in what looks like a diamond-shaped club. Their stance is hostile, as if they're ready to attack.

My creature displays its crest and flashes its beautifully coloured body at them. The wolf-like creatures seem intimidated by this. One of them flees the area, while the other two move back slowly. They are quite large compared to my creature, so I cannot quite understand why they are so intimidated. One bite from these beasts, and my creature would be down.

One of the black wolf creatures moves towards me, ignoring my creature. As it draws near, my creature leaps onto its back and sinks its small canines. Then it drops to the ground and returns to its 'displaying' position, still hissing. The wolf creature instantly falls to the floor, howling as if it's in pain. The bite from my creature seems to have injected venom into its victim, as it doesn't take long for the menacing beast to tumble to the ground. For such a small creature, my companion sure packs a punch. I'm glad it's on my side.

The other wolf-like creature flees the area with no hesitation, leaving me speechless and grateful. My creature had actually protected me against great danger. I can't believe how it took on three creatures much larger and seemingly more aggressive than itself. I was amazed at how something so small had beaten something bigger. *Must be the colouration of its skin that makes it look intimidating*, I surmise.

Limping down the path with a smirk on my face, I feel relieved and somewhat happy that I found this creature. I also feel very safe. I still can't believe or understand why this creature is so loyal to me. But I am very glad. The entire situation seems surreal.

As much as I am pleased to have this creature with me, I start to feel lonely and empty. Wild thoughts race through my head.

CHAPTER 6

In Deep Thought Again

'Wow, why am I feeling like this again?'

I feel so empty being on my own, with an unknown creature that doesn't talk back but only ogles me and wags its tail. I can find no meaning to my being here; my mind feels cloudy, and my thoughts are depressing. I feel devastated about that poor man who died. Why did he deserve that? It wouldn't have been bad to have some company. Still, though, everything has a positive side. I'm alive, and I'm in a world I could only dream about. This place is just incredible.

I sit down on a rock. I'm tired of walking and getting nowhere.

'What is this?'

The rock looks like a rock, but it has a very comfortable cushion layer. This is one of the things that freaks me out about this world. *I could just fall asleep here. How tranquil is that view.*

Stretched out in front of me are two different areas, each reached by separate pathways. Soon, I will have to take one of the paths. For now, I will rest my legs, as my knees still pain me.

I press my eyelids softly, trying to visualise the perfect life with the perfect woman. My thoughts actually feel real. She is pressing her face against my naked chest, her arms wrapped around my body and her legs snuggled against mine. We feel the warmth of each other's bodies. She's whispering that she can hear my heart beating hard, thumping away. Looking down, I see a smile on her face. She's so beautiful. In my dream, my love for her is strong, and I would do anything to give her a smile.

I hate these daydreams. They're meaningless and pointless. Why am I wasting so much of my precious time thinking about someone who isn't in my life – someone who I'll never see or meet? I am destined to be alone. Why do I keep thinking about the same girl? It's like I have seen her before. But I know I've seen her – in my dreams.

'Snap out of it. She does not exist. It's just my imagination.' I shake my head.

My eyelids are still tightly closed. I don't feel tired. I don't feel anything against my skin, no breeze. I can't hear anything either.

'Am I asleep?'

I don't think so.

'I'm talking to myself, right?' *Or am I?*

I don't feel my lips moving.

I should have saved him; Rick was his name. But there was nothing I could do. I tried my best. How could I have saved him when I don't know how to save anyone? My knowledge in medicine is okay and I can do basic CPR, but here the biology is not the same. He seemed to have been poisoned, so even if I'd tried to revive him, I would have needed an antidote to save him. I need to stop beating myself up over his death; it wasn't my fault.

At least I got to know him a bit. He seemed like a kind and very courteous man. All he wanted was peace in his life. He asked me to keep his backpack as it may come to use. But out of respect for him, I haven't even opened it to check what's inside. I will hold onto it for a while longer before checking its contents. He also mentioned that it was his lucky backpack and that he'd had it for years.

Time passes, and I presume my creature is still here at my side. I'm deep in thought and very relaxed. I've let go of my fears of this place. It's actually tranquil here – nothing to fear. My creature is kind of my protection in this world. Without it, I would have probably died back there. As for the flying creatures, I just have to avoid getting their attention.

I wonder how they noticed Rick. Did he scream to try to get their attention when they flew past? I wouldn't have thought a majestic creature like that would be interested in human flesh. What caused it to attack him is a mystery. Thinking about it, I should have asked him, as I would have learnt what not to do.

What's done is done. I can't ask him anything, and I can't bring him back. So far I have learnt nothing from my existence in this place. It's like trying to solve a broken puzzle or a puzzle with missing pieces.

Am I missing something? *Think, Michael, think.*

My creature is so loyal to me. That's another question. It helped me back there, and it would have given its life to save mine. The thing is, it has no idea what I am. It actually seems to think I'm its master of some kind. Why haven't I seen any other creatures like this? Is it meant to be following me somewhere? Is it part of the missing piece of the puzzle? I have so many unanswered questions. The big problem is they will stay unanswered, as I have no one here to answer them for me. All I've been doing is guessing, and this has led me nowhere so far.

What if this whole scenario is trying to send me a very important message – maybe that I should change jobs and start a new life? Change my sorry excuse of a house to a more comfortable one. It's funny how we end up in these situations. What wrong have I done to deserve such a loathsome life? Maybe I did something terrible in the past, before I was born. Maybe I was a murderer in a past life and this life was my punishment for the pain I'd caused others.

'Michael, stop talking like that; keep positive.'

Positive is such a good word. It carries so much meaning and is useful if used in the right context. If you are positive, anything can happen in life. Being negative only brings you down and makes you feel depressed. Not accepting that you can do more in life is not an excuse but pure laziness. Nothing is bad. Look out the window. Look at all the structures humankind has built and all the daily inventions we live with.

Back home, I have four best friends who will always be in my heart. They have done so much for me, but at times, they've given me a hard time. And I've done the same to them. That's what friends do. They don't play with your feelings or play childish mind games.

I wonder what my friends are doing as I sit here moping about my life. Two of them have loving partners. One of them has gone through so much pain and stuck by my other friend all the way when he was hospitalised and in a coma. He died twice and fought his way back to his old self. His loving partner stayed by his side, reminding his two young gorgeous girls that he was their loving dad and always staying positive, even when it looked like there was no hope. *That is the type of dedication you need from a loving partner*, I tell myself. She is very sweet and loving towards her family and friends. When I have an issue, I go to her for advice, and she calmly helps me without a second thought.

One of my other two friends is troubled. He hasn't yet found himself and is unhappy in his life. He is alone and will not let anyone in. We all try to give him advice, but sometimes it's for naught. He drinks too much, and as much as he knows how bad it is for him, he still does it. This pains all of us, as we are all quite close to each other. We never say how much we love each other. But our actions say what words should say.

My other mate is on his computer, no doubt, or taking care of his three sweet children. He keeps himself to himself, and sometimes he can push people away, as he cares too much but does not show it.

How can I forget Susan? She lives with her two beautiful children, and she is one of the kindest, most pleasant people anyone could meet. Her actions speak much louder than words. She helps so many people in her daily routine. Yet she never asks for anything in return. She is forgiving and peaceful. It takes a lot to see her angry. I've known her for around eight years now, and I have never seen her get angry. Lovely gal.

Real friends are hard to come by. But if you do come by them, you should never let them go. Most people lose their friends when they get in relationships, and this is so wrong. What can you do? Absolutely nothing. In my experience, this happens mostly with women, but I could be wrong. I've made lots of friends in my lifetime. But the ones I have now have been there for a very long time and will be there for life. I definitely need to get out of here, so I can catch up with them all again. It's been a while since we have spent quality time together.

I'm starting to understand why I'm here, but I'm still lost. I still think I have no purpose in life, and I'm still bringing myself down.

I've been here for a while, and I've been thinking too much. This is quite a comfortable rock indeed – this rock situated between two paths. 'Wake up!' I snap out of my miserable slumber and stand up, faced with a choice of what path to take.

CHAPTER 7

The Right Path: Which Path to Take?

The path splits into two. It doesn't make a difference which path I take, as I am not sure what lies ahead. Looking into the distance to the left side of the path, all I can see is mist covering the ground, like a low fog. Beyond that, I see what look like mountains and snow and a large icy pond with some different kinds of trees. I'm rather tempted to go that way; it would be interesting to see what's there.

To the right side of the path, I see what looks like different kinds of trees, all lined up in perfect rows. Then in the distance, I see woodland and a couple of valleys, as well as a huge open terrain and herds of some kind of animals. Flying creatures swarm the area, different kinds, all looking like they are competing for their territory. I see literally thousands of them, some of them looking like tropical birds.

The bleeding from the cut on my face earlier has stopped, but my grazed knees still pain me. My creature is still by my side and patiently waits for me to decide which path to take. It rubs itself against the side of my leg, wagging its tail.

'Which path shall I take, little dude?'

The creature wags its tail.

I wish it could give me advice, as I'm clueless where to go next. But I need to make my own choice.

Still, I cannot decide. One part of me says take the right path. There, I can have a look at the diversity of creatures. And maybe I can find the way out of here. It seems like the better path to take. As it stands, nothing is getting me out of here. I'm still as lost as I was when I first got here, with no notion of a way out of here and no clue as to what I'm doing.

The choice I make could affect a lot, although there is no right or wrong here.

Rarrrrr.

'What's up, little dude?'

Is it trying to say something? I think it's just getting bored. I must move on.

I'm very tempted to look inside the backpack to see what Rick had in there, but I won't open it just yet. I must be patient and wait.

I contemplate my choice. I pause for a minute and then tell myself, *Think for a second. Let your mind take you places. Ask yourself!*

Have I ever been faced with a choice before? The right choice always makes sense of course. But most people end up making the wrong choices. Sometimes, the wrong choice could be an easy way out. Do I learn from my mistakes? *Usually not.* Most people keep repeating the same old mistakes, especially when it comes to relationships. It's very rare that a person makes the right choice the first time round.

The worst thing for me is that I end up giving advice to people, advice that has come from previous experience. But instead of listening, they take the wrong path. Then they get angry with me for telling them what they don't want to hear and detach themselves from our friendship while they make the mistake. But eventually, their mistake haunts them, and they come running back, realising I was right in the first place and that they should have taken my advice.

'Hmmmmmmm.'

I keep delaying my choice. If I had a coin, I would simply flip it. But on this occasion, I have no coin, so I remain undecided.

I talk to my creature as if it's human. 'Tell me where to go, little dude. Pllllleaaaaasssssseeeee.'

It continues to wag its tail. Who knows what it is thinking? I don't even know what I'm thinking. I know my problem – I'm too engrossed in my thoughts.

I know what I should be thinking though. 'Choose!' I can't stand here all day; it's boring the hell out of me. But at the same time, I'm very hesitant. If only I could take both paths at once. Never in life can you take too many paths; no path is unachievable. But that's still avoiding my journey and the chance that I'll get out of here.

Left path it is. 'Come on, boy. Let's get going.'

I have no idea what gender my creature is. Maybe I will find out at some point.

As I start my journey, I still have doubts. Perhaps I should turn back and take the other path.

I keep walking. Hedges, all with the same red leaves and swarming with the same weird insects, tower on either side of me. I decide to take a closer look at the insects. They're the size of a housefly and bear four long, transparent, delicate wings, seeming to move in a repeated effortless motion, making them master gliders as they gracefully sit there in mid-air. Their bee-shaped bodies are yellow, and as they don't have stingers, they don't seem to be harmful. Four curvy thin red stripes lie across their abdomen. On the other hand, the thorax is black and looks hard. On earth, insects have an exoskeleton, so I presume these insects are the same or similar. They're nice looking little insects. But still, I don't want to get too close. The insects go about their business swarming around the hedge, and they don't seem to feel threatened by me at all.

The path is no longer going downhill, and I'm not gaining elevation either. I've also noticed that the path seems to have been constructed by some sentient being. The road is made of tiny pebbles cemented together. But who or what would have made this path? I keep walking, my creature still following me. The thick fog is only up to my knees. I stop and think. *What if I stray off the path?!* But looking ahead, I see that the fog never goes over the hedges, so I should be okay if I keep walking within them, at least until I get to the snowy area. I am certain that, when I was deciding which path to take, I'd seen no mist or fog in that area.

I kneel down very slightly to brush my hand against the fog. It doesn't seem cold or wet. I wonder if it's just some kind of smoke. I take my chances and bend over and take a deep breath of the fog. It has no effect on me, and it definitely doesn't smell like smoke. It looks really clean, and breathing it was actually a pleasure to my lungs, as it seemed very fresh.

I can only see the tip of my creature's crest as it follows me. It looks like a long path to the snowy area. It must be cold there. The thick layer of snow reminds me of winter back home. The mountain looks spectacular, soaring over the land beneath. I parade slowly, still limping. But I continue on; I can't stop now. Looking back, I can see the beginning of this path, but I can't see beyond as the hedges on either side are gigantic compared to me.

I wonder if anyone will be able to hear me. 'Helllooooooooooo.' All I hear is a soft echo.

Walking along, I whistle, as I have nothing else to do. For once, I'm not daydreaming but just gazing at the beautiful view ahead. I've never been somewhere like this before. The mountain is gargantuan from this view. It looks down on the world beneath its feet, laughing, as nothing compares to its enormous size. Its height towers over the blue clouds. It seems it would make Everest look tiny. I wouldn't dare to even attempt to climb it. First of all, I have no gear. And secondly, I wouldn't be able to cope with such a climb.

'What if the way out of here is behind those mountains?'

Surely whoever has put me in this world has not given me such a hard task.

'I hope not.'

Imagine how long that would take me. It doesn't matter; I'm definitely not climbing that.

As I get closer to the snowy area, I realise the temperature is still quite warmish and slightly humid. The hedges grow till the end of this path and are much aligned and stop where the path ends. This has definitely been constructed by someone. The hedges look like they have been planted and cultivated. It seems like some kind of game.

I stop at the edge of the path, kneel down, and place my palm on the snow. I'm utterly baffled. 'It cannot be snow,' I assert, as if my creature will understand my incredulity. 'It's warm.'

I grab a handful of the stuff and roll it into a ball. It compacts and feels like snow. I look closely at a small bit of it in my palm. I see tiny branches of what looks like ice coming out of other branches of 'ice', making a similar shape to that of a snowflake. It looks exactly the same. I stand back up and place my right foot on the warm snow. It sinks a little, as if I'm on a layer of deep snow.

The mountain itself isn't that far away; a lake lies ahead and some more of those weird trees I encountered earlier. The lake is steaming, which means the water must be hot. The steam has a green light shining through it. I struggle to the edge of the lake, as the 'snow' slows me down dramatically. I hesitate before touching the water, realising this could scorch my hand. Instead, I just gawk at this magnificent view, still trying to figure out what prevents this snow from melting. The temperature of the water must be at boiling point, as the water bubbles vigorously.

I try to see the bottom of the lake. I can't see much past the bubbling, but I can observe the translucent green light, giving the whole lake an incandescent look. I imagine what the lake would look like if it was nighttime. At the same time, I wonder where the light is coming from! The sky is orange. Why isn't the lake reflecting the sky?

I move around the edge of the lake to get to the base of the mountain, being careful not to fall into the water. I grab a handful of the snow in the palms of my hands, roll it into a solid compact snowball, and let it go into the lake. It just gracefully sinks. It doesn't melt at all.

With no hesitation, my creature jumps into the water, making a loud splash.

'Lil dude, come back!' I call. *Damn, I wonder why it did that.*

I sit on the snow and wait for it patiently, as I don't think it's left me. Maybe it felt like a swim. Or maybe the water is its home. *How can it withstand the heat of the water?* I cannot lose the only thing keeping me sane in this world.

A few minutes pass, and suddenly I can see the creature swimming towards the bank, using its tail like crocodiles do to swim. It moves its tail from left to right, propelling itself forward. It seems to have caught something. As it comes up to the shore, it struggles to get on the bank, as clutched between its jaws is some kind of lake creature. It looks like a fish. The creature nudges the fish towards me – as if it caught it for us. This doesn't look like the normal fish we get in our oceans. Rather, it seems to have miniature undeveloped limbs, and a large fin protrudes from its back. The fin itself looks razor sharp, and I figure it's used for protection. The gills on each side of its face would help it breathe under water, and it's a beautiful shade of silver with a small bit of gold etched on its sides. My creature takes a chunk out of the fish and, with its snout, pushes it near my foot. I grab the chunk and take a small nibble from it. It tastes really good, but its purple blood, now clotting on the snow, disgusts me. My creature is really enjoying the fish; it must be quite hungry. I realise this is its first meal since its transformation.

I leave the creature to it and give it time to devour the dead morsel. In the meantime, I just watch it ingest. I decide to sit down on the snow. But soon enough, I have to get back up, as it doesn't take long for the creature to dine. It licks its face with its long purple tongue and seems quite content and gorged. Its rounded belly suggests that my creature has had its fill.

'Time to move on.' I walk relatively slowly, as I'm still limping. But I don't feel too much pain. Straying away towards the mountain, which isn't that far away, I look back. I can see the remains of the dead carcass and the snow around it purple from its blood. My footprints are visible, as are those of my creature, and I see too the trail of its tail. I can guarantee these will be here later, as the snow doesn't seem to melt at all. In front of me, the huge mountain towers, shadowing the whole area. At its foot, I spot a hole about the size of a kitchen cupboard. Maybe it's a cave.

'Hey, little dude, shall we go in?'

Rarrrr. Rarrrrrrrrrrr.

I take that as a yes. Placing my hands on either side of the inside of the hole, I push myself into the cave, watching my step and making sure not to bang my head. '*Wow.* Look at this place!' It's like nothing I've seen before. A short wide passage with a ceiling made of red sparkling crystals, spreads out before me, and light reflects off the crystals.

Placing my hands on the cave's wall, I find it hard and transparent, like thick jelly; it's slightly damp from the cave's humidity. The floor is made of a hard rock substance with golden bits encrusted in the rock. *Is it solid gold?* I scratch the surface hard with my key, and it breaks off easily, leaving a dust of gold and rock around the scratch. 'If this cave was back home, it would be mined.' I tell my creature. This place is absolutely breathtaking.

As I walk through the cave, the walls get narrower and the ceiling gets lower, but there is still enough space for me to stay upright.

At the end of the pathway, thin vines cover what seems to be a red door. I can vaguely make out a number on the door.

'How strange.'

I take a hold of a couple of the vines and pull and tug, so I can clear them away from this door.

CHAPTER 8

Back Home. Or Am I?

Excitement stirs within me.

'What the hell?' I gasp. Is this my way out of this world? Now that I've cleared away the vines, I'm standing in front of what looks like the front door of my house, number 47. 'Definitely my house.' This is the same tacky door with the red paint peeling and showing the green paint underneath; it's unmistakably the same exact door.

I fish my keys from my pocket and gently slide the key in the hole. My hands tremble as I turn the key to the right.

A distinguishable clicking noise sounds.

The lock clicks open, and I push the door gently, peeping through the gap as I open it wider. I see the hallway that leads to my kitchen. The mat as I walk in looks quite muddy. I can barely see the welcome sign printed on it. I step inside and close the door behind me, uncovering the coat rack on the wall. Three coats are hanging from the rack, and beneath it is the tall bronze bucket where I usually place my umbrella. I walk farther inside. The beige carpet is stained. A door to my right leads to the downstairs toilet, and the one beyond that, to a staircase leading to the upstairs bathroom and bedroom.

I walk straight through to the kitchen, through an archway made of bricks, which looks like its falling apart. In the kitchen, I see a round table made of oak in the middle of the room; on the table, a patterned glass fruit bowl. It contains no fruit but, rather, a couple of paper clips and empty sweet wrappers. The chairs don't match the table but are the antique-looking, made of metal with a wooden base to sit on and a wooden back rest. The metal is rusted and very old.

The cupboards are ancient, and most of the doors are missing handles. I open the cutlery drawer. The handle comes off in my hand as the screws have come off from the inside. The slightly rusted sink is full of dirty plates and a quarter of the way filled up with water. The tap drips slowly, but as the drain is clogged, it's filling up. And the water smells stagnant. The smell forces me to heave as I walk past it. My creature seems to not like being here, as it remains lying on the mat near the front door.

I feel disgusted being in my own home. Even the tiles are cracked, and in the crevices of the cracks, black muck is building up. The fridge needs to be changed as the sides are quite oxidised and the door handle is badly damaged. The cooker is new; I bought it a few months ago. The old one stopped working completely and was a bit of a hazard, as it leaked gas. That nearly put me in hospital. I remember it as if it was yesterday. I was cooking, and I lit a cigarette. The light triggered a small explosion. I look at the wall behind the cooker; it's still charred from that incident. I really haven't had time to paint over it. The rest of the wall is a bluish colour, and the kitchen window is the old wooden type.

I leave the kitchen area through the archway to the hallway and head up the stairs, the wooden floorboards creak as I climb. Straight ahead, I see the bathroom door, white but scratched all over, revealing the wood underneath. The bathroom tiles are dark blue, and most of them are broken. Disgusting grime covers the sink basin, and the build-up around the taps is enough to put me off being in here. The cold tap drips, as it doesn't close properly. The toilet is surprisingly clean inside, but the bottom is layered in dust and grime.

It's not that I don't enjoy cleaning, but when I live in such bad conditions already, I can't be bothered to improve on the cleanliness of the place – especially when I'm renting. The least I expect is for the taps to be fixed. I've only been living here for around two months, and most of the grime was already here when I moved in. I was in a rush to find somewhere new, and this place didn't seem like a bad idea at the time. The bath is spotless, as I scrubbed it inside and out a week ago. Just some water marks on the taps.

I need a new house; this one is unbearable, and I can't live like this anymore. I get out of the bathroom and head into the bedroom. It smells nice in here, but it's very cold, a result of my not being able to close the window – another thing I've reported to my landlord but have not heard back about. I lie on the bed for a few minutes, as the mattress is not old and cost me a great part of my monthly salary; it's very comfortable, and I could lie here all day long, as I feel snug. The cushiony feel of the pillows and the sweet smell of lavender make me feel tired. I shouldn't sleep, so I get off the bed and walk over to the window to look outside. As I get closer, I can feel that the carpet beneath the window is soaked with water; a squidgy sound accompanies every step I take. The window sill soaking wet, and water drips off the side. Outside, the cats are roaming free in the street, as it is not raining anymore. A few people are walking down the street. The neighbours must have gone out when the thunderstorm halted. They don't drive, so they walk to the store. They are quite old pensioners, and they seem so lovely holding hands – a very sweet sight.

I step away from the window and open my wardrobe to get some fresh clothes. The wardrobe is empty. A surge of anger rushes through me as realisation dawns – I must still be in an illusion.

I thought I'd left that world I was in. I close the wardrobe and run back downstairs into the kitchen. I open the fridge and all the cupboard doors

– all empty. In the time that I was upstairs, notes have covered the front of the fridge. They all say the same thing – 'Get out.' 'Get out. 'Get out.' Small notes all the same cover the fridge door.

I scratch my head with frustration. 'What does that mean?' I open the back door, which is situated in the kitchen. The back entrance is blocked; wooden planks nailed together in a shabby way prevent my exit. Sprayed on the wood graffiti style is the same message. 'Get out.' But why?

I can't think at this stage, but I need to do what the message says.

I scream at the top of my voice, as I don't know what is going on. My anger is building. I grab the chair closest to me and throw it across the kitchen, hitting and breaking one of the kitchen cupboards.

'Michael, calm down,' I say to myself. I rub my face in disbelief. What is this screwed-up situation?

I walk straight to the front door. My creature still lies there sleeping on the mat. It looks very peaceful. I place my hand on its head to wake it up. It slowly opens its eyelids and its jaws widen in a yawn. It stands on all fours and stretches out.

Rarrrrrrrrrrrrrrrrrrrrrrrrrrrrrrrrrrrrrrrrrrrrrrrrrrrrrrrrrrrrrrrrrrrr.

'Come on, little dude. This place is a complete joke. We have to head out.'

I feel quite sorry I interrupted its sleep. But we have to leave this place. This has opened my eyes, and I've learnt a clear message here – Mike, you definitely need to move house. You cannot keep living like this.

Coming here was not a good idea. I realise this as I open the front door. I can't believe my eyes. The cave, the snowy area has all disappeared.

'What is going on?'

No point in shouting; no one can hear me. Why has it all changed? Where is the cave? So much frustration.

I stare at an ocean, purple and apparently very calm. In the short distance, I can see where I came from, although the snowy area has disappeared and the mist on the path is gone. This cannot be the lake I came across earlier. The water does not bubble at all. I kneel down and dip my fingers in the water to check if it is hot. *Hmm warm but not hot!* The place is flooded. The landscape has changed dramatically. *But why?* I decide to get myself wet, and I jump into the ocean.

CHAPTER 9

Deep Ocean Purple

As I sink to the bottom, I feel a slight pressure from the jump, mostly in my ears. My creature has followed me, and it's wagging its tail from left to right to swim, its limbs held back. I flap my arms and legs with all my strength to try to swim upwards. It's no use, as I just keep sinking. Holding my breath, I wonder how long this will last. Air bubbles escape from my mouth and nostrils as I struggle.

I land on my feet on the silt that makes up the bottom of the ocean. The ocean looks purple from down here, and my visibility is very clear as I open my eyes. I can see up from the surface quite clearly. The huge orange sun, although it looks very rippled, is still perfectly visible.

I see different types of rocks that look like coral, and shoals of tiny multicoloured creatures swim all around me. They look quite similar to our fish, but a lot of them seem to have limbs. Some have colourful spikes. And some other species have tentacles. In the distance to my left, there seems to be a predator, hunting for smaller creatures. It's about the size of a bus, and its head is long and flat with a wide jaw accommodating hundreds of double serrated sword-like teeth. I must be careful, as I can't be eaten by this. My walk through this ocean seems to be in slow motion. It's not like water at home; it feels thicker.

I'm not short of breath. I have been down here for a few minutes now; I've taken a few paces forward, and I've been scanning the area. It seems like I don't have to worry about getting to shore quickly. I might as well explore a bit. I reach down to the seabed and grab a handful of the blue silt. It feels like a handful of sugar, and it glimmers; in fact, the entire seabed shimmers and seems very magical. I let go of the handful of silt, and it sparkles as it slowly sinks to the seabed. I move towards the shoreline, grabbing onto rocks to propel myself forward. On closer inspections, the 'rocks' look more like sponges. I realise they must be alive, as the first one I grabbed moved away slightly.

It's going to take a while to get to shore, as I've only managed about ten steps forward. Yet my creature, swimming along in front of me, seems to be enjoying this swim. I keep a sharp eye on the predator's movement, as I would not be able to withstand its attack.

My movement forward attracts fish-type creatures. They swarm around me – a bit too close. A shoal of about 200 fiery red fish with bright green stripes, no bigger than my thumbnail, approach me. They have eyes on each side of their brightly coloured faces, and look very cute. They must feed on some kind of vegetation or microscopic creatures, as they don't seem to have teeth. They are very curious little creatures, neighbouring me as I edge forward. My creature darts through them, getting a mouthful of these fish and making them scatter. Around me, I see quite a large number of vegetation. Most of it looks like reeds – although they aren't reeds, as reeds usually live above water.

I start noticing that my creature's interest has been heightened by a large boulder. It pushes the rock with its snout. I move forward and grab hold of this rock. I help my creature. I push with my shoulder and arms to move the rock. Our work doesn't take long; the rock moves, stirring up the silt from the bottom of the ocean and revealing what my creature was interested in.

Eggs of some sort – a clutch of thirteen eggs. They are covered in a zigzag pattern and look quite precious. What creature would have laid its eggs under the rock? I take hold of one of the eggs. It's rather heavy and very smooth – like porcelain, delicate to the touch. Yet a rock has been sitting on them, so I cannot imagine they break that easily. I see no point in trying to crack one open down here, as I try to throw it to the ground and nothing happens; it doesn't travel fast enough to hit the seabed with enough force to break. My creature seems to have quite an interest in these eggs. Wondering why, I decide to hold onto one of the eggs, I place it inside the backpack. After pushing the rock back over the rest of the clutch, I keep moving, seeing some wonderful wildlife down here. And I don't feel the need to breathe. I'm still holding my breath, but I don't need to let it out at all.

It doesn't take long for the flat-beaked creature wading my way to notice my presence. My creature darts straight for it and steers the flat-beaked creature away from me. It swims round to its side and attacks from underside, biting the beast's unprotected belly. The flat-beaked creature seems to be struggling as my creature clutches onto it; eventually, the poison sets in and kills it. The beast sinks to the bottom, leaving a dark trail of black blood resembling ink behind. The blood forms a cloud and just floats there, building up into a thicker cloud as the beast bleeds.

I try to signal to my creature to come back; it circles the dead creature a few times and eventually swims back to me. This thing is not afraid of anything. *Well done, my boy*, I think to myself. I look ahead, and the water is getting shallower, but it's still a bit of a trail to get there. And I cannot exactly run in this. I'm plodding along the bottom of the cleanest ocean I have ever seen. It seems the water is oxygenated, as quite a few areas of the seabed are releasing bubbles; that usually meant oxygen, but in this world, it could be anything. Could be methane, usually made from decaying plants and dead animals, for all I know. Staring at it, I feel like I'm in a huge aquarium.

I feel like a dad taking my kid out to the playground as my creature swims through the bubbles. I think it's really enjoying itself. It floats up into the bubbles and swims back down and through the powerful jets. How sweet!

The shoreline doesn't look that far away. But still, it will take me some time to get there. I decide to try to take a leap forward. I throw my arms back to get momentum, and as they come forward, I leap. I don't make much progress, as my jump isn't that high and I'm pulled back down; the gravitational force is quite harsh here. My legs feel tired, and I'm aching.

I approach an area full of tall ocean grass, swaying gently in sequence with the ocean's movement. It doesn't make sense that this vegetation is floating up and, yet I'm not floating at all. In fact, it's the complete opposite. I decide to go around the grass. I stretch my arm out and pass my palm through the grasses.

My creature swims through them; it's not afraid of anything. It seems to be familiar with the creatures and plants down here. The geology of this place is interesting and must be rich in minerals, as everything here seems to be flourishing. The food chain must work in the same way as it does back home. The plants must be getting their energy from the sun above and growing with help from the rich nutrients in the silt. Beyond the tall grass, I see nothing but ocean, rich with jets of bubbles breaking out of the ground violently, and the odd fish no larger than my hand.

My weight is lifting as I approach the shoreline, maybe because the water is getting shallower. Even the silt is changing colour. The water is so purple that I can't discern the exact colour. It feels very much like sand, is quite dull to the naked eye, and doesn't seem to have the minerals needed to grow large thickets of ocean grass; this area is completely baron – apart from the small flowers growing here. *Flowers under water?* How strange. Everything is different here, so nothing's unexpected.

I open my mouth and accidentally swallow a bit of the water. It doesn't taste salty; rather, it tastes quite bitter. It's not very nice; I definitely won't do that again.

Slowly but surely, I'm nearly there. I wonder if the path I saw from the other side is the same path I was on before. Before I jumped in the water, it looked like there was no mist on it, so I can't be sure. As I walk, my head comes out of the water, and I can actually see the path ahead of me. Sure enough, it's the same one, with hedges on either side.

I cough hard and start feeling nauseous. 'I wonder if it's the water I swallowed,' I muse. I rush to the path and sit down. Removing my backpack, I rest my back against the hedge. My creature sits here next to me. I look at it. What's happening? I start to suffer with double vision. My vision is getting worse. My eyesight is blurry, and my head is feeling heavy. I pull both my hands up in front of my face; they look distorted.

Slowly, I'm blacking out.

I'm dying? ... What's happening?

'Goodbyeee, littttle du—

Rarrrrr.

My vision is now going black; I can't hold on for much longer. I lay myself down on the ground.

CHAPTER 10

Noeleen

I wake up with a sudden fright. My vision is blurry, and I'm yawning. I rub my eyes and forehead, rubbing my eye shadow and foundation onto my hands. My vision is slowly coming to par, and the first thing I notice is the grass beneath me.

'Oh my god. Where am I?'

I sit up and find myself on turquoise grass, dressed in a black dress. And I'm still wearing a gold-plated costume jewellery necklace.

I shut my eyes, hoping I'm just dreaming, open them, and blink a few times. 'What is this place? This is no dream.'

I have no idea what to do next.

The last thing I remember, I was out with my girls; we partied all night. Some guys kept trying to get with us, but I remember pushing away any guy who came close to me. In fact, one guy pulled me towards him and tried to kiss me, and I was struggling. My friend Martina came up to him and kicked him in the leg to get him off. He was very drunk, and he wouldn't let go. That's when I kneed the guy in the private area, and he instantly let go, calling me names and saying he would find me when I get out of the club. I went up to the bouncer and told him about the guy, and the bouncer kicked him out of the club. We laughed about the situation and continued drinking as normal.

Around three in the morning, we decided to call it a night, but I can't remember leaving the club. I must have had a lot to drink.

I class myself as very caring. I like things to be perfect, and I take great care of the way I look. My friends all say I am quite the party animal, but I'm still the quietest of the group. From the time I wake up in the morning, I dedicate time to whatever I am doing, and I like to finish strong and in a good fashion. I can be quite opinionated and stand my ground when it comes to what I believe in. There's nothing wrong with being like this. In fact, it's good to stand up for yourself - even for someone like me who's so relaxed all the time.

I don't usually like to express my feelings openly. In fact, I do bottle a lot of problems inside, and when I'm angry, I tend to take it out on myself, rather than on my friends or family. As for relationships, I'm not really that trusting, because usually when I trust, I get stabbed in the back. But I know that life is like that, and there is nothing anyone can do about it. In my experiences, guys only want me for my body. All I want is a guy who will see me as his lover and his best friend and not as a quick one-night stand.

Buying expensive gifts is *not* the best thing any guy can do for me. The most important thing of all is that he respects me enough not to want to sleep with me on the first or second date. I want a guy who will love every flaw in me, someone I can open up to, instead of bottling my problems inside. I need a man in my life, not a childish boy. What is the point in getting with someone just for sex?! It doesn't make sense; my body is not to be used. If a guy can't see me for a month before sex, then he is not the guy for me.

So now what do I do? I'm somewhere I've never been before. I'm not sure what I'm doing here, and I have no idea where to go. Maybe I should at least walk around and see what's here. I feel that lump in my throat that I used to get whenever I had to go up the dark stairs to the attic all alone to find something for my mom, and my heart is racing. Being in a situation where I have no control always brings this feeling. I really don't want to move from this spot. I don't think I have a choice though.

I have no bag on me. I must look really bad. My hair feels knotted as I brush my fingers through it to try to get it to a half-decent state. I stand up in an upright position and brush my dress down from top to bottom. For some odd reason, I am wearing trainers with this dress. I'm very grateful that I'm not wearing heels. Walking in heels wouldn't be such a good idea; the grass feels way too soft, and the heel would get stuck in the thick turf.'

I have woken up in an open field, and surrounding me are trees in the not too far-off distance. I scan the area around me and notice a briefcase. I walk to it and open it. Nothing but a note is inside. The note says, 'He is here.'

Who is here? I wonder. What is going on? And why is a strange briefcase with nothing inside it here? I ignore my questions and start moving slowly towards an opening in the trees. I'm not sure where it will lead me to, but I'm sure I should get out of this area. I look down at the grass; it seems as if something has been dragged to the opening I'm facing.

I walk cautiously. As I follow the trail, I notice some kind of feather, which I pick up. It seems to be made of a hard substance, yet it is very light and quite large. The feather must belong to a creature that lives here, I conclude. Something must have gone terribly wrong in this area. I move more quickly towards the opening.

Suddenly, I realise I'm running towards what seems to be a dead body. *Oh my god! Someone died here!* I get close to the man; he looks very pale, and he is definitely dead. I wonder what happened. I start contemplating how he died. I check his pulse to make sure he isn't alive. Someone was near him for sure, as his hands are both on his chest, one on top of the other, and a nice colourful bunch of leaves have been placed on his chest. I also notice that a nice thick amount of turf, moss, and collected leaves is under his head.

'This is starting to freak me out.'

I start screaming, ignoring any dangers that could be lurking around me. *'Helllooo?'* I stay silent for a few seconds. 'Can anyone hear me?' Why won't anyone answer me?

I cower near the dead body for a while, as I'm not sure what to do next. I sit down and start thinking. Why am I here? I have no idea where I am, and I'm all alone, but someone else must be here. I push myself back up from the sitting position and continue walking. The grass looks like it's been walked on. I should follow this and keep going straight. I look around me, seeing tree after tree and feeling quite helpless in this strange place. I keep walking, getting startled at the slightest sound. In the distance, I see a tree with some markings on it. I slowly walk towards it. The markings look like scratch marks.

Like someone left a message.

'Noeleen, turn left.' That's all it says.

I wonder what this message means. I feel very uneasy, and my hands are shaking. I have no idea what is going on. Why is my name engraved on this tree? Surely no one here knows me. I am very volatile and weak. I start moving again. I notice a tree pulsating, which makes me jump out of my skin. A tear trickles down my left cheek. I've never been like this in my life. I'm all alone in a strange world.

Is that an opening up ahead?

About 500 metres away from me, I make out what looks like an opening in this thick forest. I have never been in an area with so many trees, and I would never be talked in to going and exploring any forest. The even scarier part is that these trees look nothing like the trees back home. And the fruit on them look so strange. I don't even dare think what they taste like.

I pick up my pace, wanting to get to the opening. I hope something better is on the other side. My fear elevates by the second. *Not far now*, I tell myself. Each tree I pass means the opening is getting closer to me, and a small feeling of relief crosses over me. So many feelings are going through me at the moment – fear and uncertainty at the head of the pack. I see no sense in my being in this place.

I place one palm on the trunk of a tree just on the outskirts of the forest and gaze out into the opening. In front of me stands a huge row of bushes and a path that splits in two. To my right, the path seems to be going uphill. And to my left, another heads downhill. I go uphill, ignoring the message on the trunk of that tree, amazed at how well the path seems to be constructed. I see boulders to the side of the lane up ahead. I don't wish to explore; I want to get out of here. I keep moving. At the top of the lane, where the path cuts off, all I can see is a huge desert with a few dead trees and a huge lake.

'Hmmm, maybe the tree was right, and I should have turned left,' I mutter.

I turn around to start walking downhill and realise how much I can see from this spot. Wow. What a view. But I'm too scared to enjoy the view for more than a second. I need to get out of this place.

'Where am I now?'

I worry my mind is going crazy. I keep asking myself the same thing out loud when no one is here. I start walking downhill. Unaware of what will happen next, I look to my sides, upwards, and behind me, contemplating every possibility I can imagine. I think skittish may be the word to describe how I feel at the moment. Also, I keep being bothered by the fact that I have no bag or any pockets. I don't have a clue what I look like.

Ahead, I see I've made it back to the split in the path. I walk to it. Great. I have to make a choice. I'm very disappointed, as it seems like I'm now faced with a riddle. I try to decide which path to take. I look towards the left path.

'Is that a body?'

Lying at the bottom of the path is a guy. 'He moved his leg.'

I determine that he must be alive and that I need to get down there as quick as possible. I pretty much run down the path. When I'm about three metres from his body, I realise something is next to the body. I can't be sure what it is. It's some kind of creature, and it's just sitting there. I have no idea how the guy ended up on the ground like that. Was it that creature? *Did it attack that man?* I'm really scared of what it might be, but I have to risk it. I cannot ignore the fact that someone else is here. *But what if that creature attacks me aswell? Might be protecting that man.* I decide to risk it.

I walk very vigilantly, and I'm sure my wariness would be evident to any observer. I take each step, pace by pace. I can't run, as doing so might frighten whatever that animal is. It might attack me, and I'll end up like that guy or worse.

I get quite close, and the creature approaches me, getting quite close. It wags its tail, looks straight up at me, and runs back to the unconscious body. This creature does not seem to feel threatened. Rather, I think it's trying to tell me something.

I walk towards the body. I kneel down and place my hand over the man's chest.

He seems to be breathing quite heavily, and his heart rate seems normal. From the colour of his face, he looks quite healthy. Handsome indeed. I look ahead along the path. I see what looks like thick snow, a lake, and a mountain. I need to get this injured man to safety. I gaze over towards the colossal mountain. *Is that a cave?*

From here, it looks like one, but I can't be sure. I grab the man by both his arms and drag his body along the snow. 'Wow, he's heavy.' I struggle to continue, but before long I can no longer do it. I am getting too tired. I decide to sit down, and I lay his head on my thighs while I rest.

Suddenly it occurs to me that the snow I'm sitting on is warm and doesn't seem to be melting. 'What is this stuff?'

I wonder who this man is. He seems stuck here as well; he is wearing a suit. His knees are badly grazed, and the trousers are torn. I get up again. I grab his arms and pull him towards the foot of the mountain. That is definitely a cave. We should be safe inside. And I will try to help him. Maybe he's in a deep sleep. But surely he would have woken up by now.

I drag his body inside the cave, not really taking any notice of what's around me. I sit the man up with his back against the wall, removing his backpack and placing it near him in the process. I stroke his face gently.

'Wake up. Please.'

Nothing.

CHAPTER 11

Wake Up

'Wake up.'

'Mmmm.'

'Hey, wake up. Are you okay?'

'Mmmmmm.'

I hear a voice telling me to wake up. My eyelids are sealed shut, and I'm not sure what's going on. I can't seem to wake up, but I can still hear her voice.

'Am ... am I ... alive?'

'Hey you're alive. Open your eyes.'

Still, I cannot open my eyes. But I can definitely hear that. She sounds amazing. Her voice is like a good tune to my ears – very soft and gentle. She's asking me to open my eyes. Is she an angel here to save me? Am I dead? I feel alive but cannot move. I'm just thinking at the moment. My leg moves slightly now and again, but that's about it. It's just a random muscle spasm.

Why is she near me? Who is she? And where has she come from? I want to see her. She'll be someone to talk to. And maybe … Who knows? Maybe, we can find our way out of this situation together. I still feel nauseous and hot – and helpless, as I can't move.

I just need to wake up because, if she leaves, I will be all alone again.

'What's …'

'What's what? I'm still here. Hello?'

Grrr. I can't finish the sentence, as my tongue is also paralyzed. My mouth is shut, and I can only manage to move it slightly. I'm not drinking that water again; that's for sure. *Say something. Hear my thoughts. I want to hear your voice.* She sounded amazing. This can't be real; the situation is very surreal, unbelievable. She sounds really sweet and young. I must be in a deep sleep, dreaming. She doesn't exist. She's just a thought – pure imagination.

I can't be sure if she's still here, although I can hear a slight noise. Is she stroking my creature? I listen closely and try to use my sense of smell. All I detect are smells of the cave – and then a faint smell of perfume. I conclude it must be hers. She must be real. I scream out loud in my mind, hoping she'll wait for me to wake up. We'll find our way out of here together.

Rarrrrrr …. Prrrrr. My creature must like her. What a relief it's still with me. I must have been knocked out for hours on that path. I wonder what my creature did all that time. Maybe it was protecting my fragile body, or maybe it went for a swim in the ocean. Thinking of the ocean somehow makes me attuned to smells, and I realise that the smells here are similar to that of the cave I was in earlier. But how? Did she drag me on the ocean bed? Or did the ocean miraculously disappear? This situation just gets stranger and stranger. I wonder if my house door is still at the end of this cave. And if it is, I hope she doesn't go through it because I will end up losing her.

So far, it seems she has not gone anywhere. It seems she's staying here with me for now. *Please, creature, stay with her. Keep her protected and make sure she doesn't leave.* Not that it can hear me. And even if it could hear me, I don't think it can understand human language anyway.

Hearing what sounds like Velcro, I realise she must be undoing the side of my backpack. No way. I can't believe she's opening it.

'What's this?'

Her voice sounds appealing. I wonder what she's found. Then I hear her make a happy noise, followed by the unmistakable sound of pages being opened. I wonder what kind of book Rick might have had.

'So you're a poet.'

She pauses, and I'm sure I can actually feel her smiling at me.

'And your name's Michael.'

Ay? That's not mine. Why does Rick's book have my name on it?

'I hope you enjoy hearing your own poems read' She says in her sweet voice.

> *My Dreams, My Thoughts*
> *Without you, I'm lost.*
> *It won't come true,*
> *Being together with you.*
> *I dream about this girl,*
> *I dream.*
> *Real it seems –*
> *Holding her tight,*
> *Then she smiles,*
> *Giving her a kiss on her cheek,*
> *Who is she?*

'Who are you talking about Michael.'

'You seem really sweet.'

That is my poem, but I did not bring my poems here. I wrote that a few days ago. This is screwed up. How would Rick have gotten hold of my poem? What else does that backpack hold? And how did the paper she was reading from still legible? I'm really getting frustrated now; I want to see what else is in the pack. Surely everything in the pack is soaked.

This girl thinks I'm sweet, I realise. I wish I could smile at her.

In fact, I wish I could just see her. I can only try to imagine what she is like. And I can't tell much about her appearance from just her voice. She sounds rather intelligent, and she seems like she has a foreign accent. The accent sounds familiar. *Think, Michael. Lift your arm up or something. Acknowledge that you can hear her. Say something. Do something.*

I try as hard as I can to fight this paralysis, but I can do nothing until the water I drank is out of my system – unless this is permanent. I really hope that's not the case. What bad timing. Why didn't she find me earlier? If only. And Rick … What's in his backpack? The poem is mine, not his. I heard her say the poem is signed with my name. How can that be?

Am I being tested or something? I start thinking about what Rick told me. I can't think of anything that points at any situation. Oh no, she is flicking through the pages.

'I'm going to read this one next' She says.

Minute to minute,
Hour to hour,
Seeing her here smiling.
Her lips taste sweet,
Quite ravishing.
I feel her breath on my chest,

As I am holding her close.
I feel like a mess,
Deep in thought.
Deeper and deeper,
She makes my world.
My heart grows stronger,
My lips are shaking.
She's the sun in my life.
Then some rain falls down.
Waiting for a sign,
The past is gone,
I'm writing in present tense.
These feelings are real.
Close in my arms she rests.
End of my lovely.

I hear her set the notebook down. 'Who is she, Michael? She must be special.' She sighs. 'Such a romantic.'

She needs to stop reading my poetry. It sounds really old-fashioned. A grown man who writes poetry. That's how I express my feelings. But these poems where made for that special girl in my head. It makes me sound so crazy. I hear the rustling sound as she turns the page over, and I don't know what's coming next.

I'm sitting here,
Thinking about that girl,
That girl I think about,
Thoughts in my head.
In the morning, from when I wake
Till the minute I close my eyes,
She's still in my thoughts.
Trying to sleep,

I'm trying to visualise,
Us two together,
Personalities synchronized,
Butterfly feeling,
Deep down in my gut,
For her, I fight.
What's her name?

'I've never had a guy write me a poem before.'

Why does she seem upset about that? *Whoever you are, I will write you a poem.* I just need to wake up first.

She flicks to the next page.

'Is this a drawing of me? What are you? Some kind of stalker?'

What? How can there be a drawing of her? I've never seen her in my life. I do not know how to draw! How did Rick know her? I really hope she doesn't leave now that she's seen that. I did not draw it. As for Rick, he and I lived 300 miles away from each other, so there's no way he could have taken my poetry, not to mention read my thoughts.

At first I thought this was real, but as time is passing by, I'm beginning to feel like I'm dreaming. I'm probably just lying on the ground on that path. She's not saying anything, so I'm not sure if she's still here. In fact, I can't hear anything. *What's going on?*

I listen for the slightest sound. All I can hear is droplets of water dripping from the ceiling onto the cave floor. If this is real, my creature has left me, and she has gone too. The other possibility is that they are both asleep, but I doubt that.

I need to say something.

'*Help.*'

I hear only the echo of my voice – nothing else. I didn't hear her footsteps walking out of the cave. I keep listening for a while, and time passes.

Finally, I hear something, like a shoe scraping on the floor. I wonder what's going on.

'Wow, I must have fallen asleep.'

She was asleep after all.

The little dude better be here when I get up from this slumber. Bet he's very restless waiting, if he's still here.

I try to envision the gal in front of me just sitting there, waiting patiently for me to wake up from this. I'm very content that she is still here. For a while, I thought she had gone back. I don't think she could leave now. Why would she want to be in this world alone? It's quite a desolate place –no other humans to seek protection from and all the dangerous creatures I've come across.

The fact she found the notebook, which I didn't even know was here, is irritating me. I really need to wake up and check it out. Hearing her narrate my poems was quite astonishing. She also thinks I'm very sweet, I remember. And she thinks I have a special someone in my life. But what does she think about that drawing of her in the pad? She hasn't really said anything about it. Yet she's still here with me.

I hear her flicking through the notebook again.

'He he he.' She's giggling to herself at something now. What the hell is she giggling at? Is it me? Something in the notebook?

Michael, you can do it. Ahhhh why can't I move? What was in that water?

'Michael, wake up!'

I actually spoke out loud. At least that will let her know I'm not dead.

'Michael? Are you awake?' she asks.

She sounds delightful. I keep trying to talk, but it's just difficult at the moment.

I hear movements and then the echo of her footsteps. *Oh no!* She's leaving. I think she's walking out of the cave. I wonder where she is going and what she intends to do on her own. *Don't go, please.* I want to say it out loud, but nothing will come out. Why can't I just call her back?

I feel a sharp devastation in my core. She hasn't even told me her name. I feel worried about her. How is she going to cope all alone?

A few minutes pass, and I hear footsteps again, this time coming towards me. Is this her again? Has she had a change of mind and decided to stay with me till I wake?

'I'm here, Michael. I got you some water to drink.'

Oh no.

'I have to wake him up somehow,' she mutters to herself.

Nooooooooooooooo! I really hope she has not been drinking the water herself.

She holds my nose and opens my mouth. I can't move to stop her. I'm helpless, and she is totally unaware of why I'm like this. The warm water slides down my oesophagus. I can taste a slight sweetness, and surprisingly, it tastes very refreshing. That water must be from that lake.

I start feeling better instantly. My legs start moving, and I feel great. A few minutes pass, and I realise I've regained my motor control. I open my eyes.

'Hi, I'm Michael,' I say, seeing her for the first time.

CHAPTER 12

The Notebook of Dreams

'I'm Noeleen. Pleased to meet you, Michael.'

I get up from my sitting position and shake her hand. My sense of touch goes wild; her skin is soft and her handshake gentle. I look into her eyes. I can't explain what I feel at this minute.

I look around the cave. The backpack is open, and the creature is sleeping.

I just stare at her, speechless.

'Hey, you can let go of my hand now.'

I instantly let go of her hand. My nerves are strong around her, and I blush as she smiles at me.

'You don't need to blush, Mike. What happened to you?'

'Long story, to be honest. I've been stuck in this world for a while now.'

'Go on. Tell me more.'

'Okay then. Sit down here.'

I sit down where I was previously sitting. I close my backpack and pat my hand on the ground next to me. She sits near me.

'Go on, Mike. Tell me what happened.'

'Are you comfortable? How do you feel?' I ask.

'Well, a bit overwhelmed by this world. I'm not sure where I am and that makes me …frightened is the word. Then I saw you, and somehow now I feel quite safe.'

'Good to hear.' I smile at her to comfort her. 'I have been in this world for a while now. I'm not sure where you've been, but I started with a desert behind me and a path going downhill. I love to explore, so I have been stopping everywhere to explore my surroundings. I ended up in an open field, helping a guy called Rick. Unfortunately, he died,' I add softly.

'Oh yes,' she replied. 'I started off in that field and followed a trail on the grass. He was just lying there dead. His name was Rick?' she asks.

'Was my briefcase still there?'

She strangely looks at me.

'Yes. And there was a note that said, "He is near."'

'Wow, Noeleen, that is really freaky. I found a note that said, "She is near."'

Was the note about her? The girl in my daydreams looks like her, but you can never know. A dream is a dream, but maybe this occasion is different.

'What happened after that, Mike?'

'Well, I spoke to Rick for a while, and he gave me his backpack, which I didn't want to open.'

'Ohhhh, I'm sorry.'

'No it's okay. I kept walking and got to a path that split into two. I took the path that led to this cave. And at the end of the cave, I found a door. Oh yeah, and I found this creature, which saved my life twice. And it seems to be following me everywhere. As for the door, get this; it led to my house. I thought I was out of this strange world. But posted on the fridge were a load of notes telling me to get out. I went to leave through the front door, and I found an ocean between me and the path back from where I'd come. I jumped into the ocean, and I could hold my breath in it forever. And then I swallowed some of the water, which made me black out. I'm not too sure how long I'd been on that path before you found me and dragged me here. That's what happened, right?'

She nodded.

'Thank god you did. To be honest, I was going crazy all by myself here.'

'What's with the notes? There was a note on a tree trunk that said to turn left and then the notebook ... Wait, you said you never opened the bag. How did your poems end up in it? Sorry, I read a few.'

'I'm not quite sure, I never put the notebook in the bag and I heard you talk. I could hear everything. I just couldn't move at all.'

'Oh. I thought you were asleep.'

'No. I was awake but paralyzed. Do you know where the notebook is?'

'Gimme a sec. I put it back in the side pocket of your backpack.'

She is so gorgeous. I catch myself staring at her as she twists around slightly to her left to find the notebook. I wonder where she came from and where she actually lives. I can't ask her too many questions. I don't want to seem rude. She keeps giggling as she rustles through the bag. She looks at me with her eyes wide open and smiles as she talks.

'It's not in the side pocket. Give me a minute, Mike.'

She grins at me, instantly giving me a warm feeling in my core. I haven't felt this feeling for a long time – over three years I would say. She seems so kind and gentle, and she's very relaxed in the way she moves.

'Hey, hey, I found it.' Excitedly, she hands me the notebook. 'Why don't you read me one of your poems, Mike?'

Is she serious? All of a sudden, I feel a tingling sensation and a sense of warmth rushing through my body. I can feel my heart pumping hard, and I feel speechless.

'Go on.' She giggles at me, smiling a large smile. Is she flirting with me?

'Okay, okay, tell you what. Close your eyes and randomly open a page, and I will read what's on it, okay?'

'Sounds fun.'

She closes her eyes, revealing her smeared eye shadow, and bites her bottom lip. She holds her hand out, instinctively trying to find the notebook. 'Help me out, Mike. I can't see.'

'Okay, here you go.' I laugh and nudge her hand with the notebook.

'Hmmmm, I choose …this page.' She opens her eyes and looks down at the notebook. 'Open it,' she says, handing it to me. 'I've done my part choosing. Now it's your turn. Don't be shy. Read.'

I turn to the page she pointed at, revealing a poem I wrote. Very hesitantly, I start reading, knowing I will stutter.

I woke up one morning

With a feeling—

I can't read it; I just start laughing. I'm really shy, especially when I'm put in this type of position – in front of a gal I hardly know. And now I'm supposed to be reading something I wrote a while ago. Although I've never seen this notebook before, I do recognise this poem. In fact, I know it by heart. I wonder where Rick got it from.

'What's the holdup, Mike? You are not getting out of this.'

I laugh nervously again. 'I'm sorry. I'm just shy and a bit embarrassed.'

'Take your time.'

She always talks with a sweet smile on her face. She places her right arm on my knee for a few seconds – which just makes it worse. But If I read it now, then this will be over and done with. I hope she won't ask me to read another.

'Okay, here we go, Noeleen. Please don't laugh.'

I swallow hard before I start and wipe the sweat off my forehead. Here it goes.

I woke up one morning,
With a feeling deep inside,
An empty feeling,
A dark feeling.
Not here beside me,
All alone,
She is never here.
A deep fear,
Sheer pain,
My heart broken,
Feeling sick,
Wishing I had never woken,
Broken to pieces,
Trying to mend,
Crying hard,
Not feeling like a man.

What for?
What did I do to deserve this?
This shadow, dark light,
Burning me deep inside.'

Somehow, I don't feel so good any more. This is a very sad poem. I remember writing this now. Who was I talking about though? This was a while ago.

'Bravo, Mike!'

'Hey, you liked it? Are you crying?'

She seems to have been touched by my poem. I can see a teardrop running down her rosy cheeks. 'Yes. Your poem really made me feel something there.'

I rub her arm to comfort her. 'It's okay, Noeleen. I'm not judging you at all here. Relax.'

She slides over and is now sitting closer to me. She sobs a bit, but I can still see a slight smile on her face. I wonder what she's thinking. It seems she likes my poetry. She must be very sensitive.

'Somehow I feel like I know you, and I feel very safe,' she says softly.

'I know, right? I was so worried about being alone here. But then you turned up, and I can't explain what I'm feeling right now.'

If only she knew what I was feeling, I doubt she would want to stick with me. Here I was again, being negative and thinking of the worst. But what if she thinks otherwise? I can't blow it just yet. I need to hide my feelings. In the past, showing feelings too soon ended what could have been magical with others.

'What are you thinking, Mike?'

If only she knew. I can't say much at this point, but I can give her the chance to see how respectful I am. Smiling big, I reply, 'Well, Miss Noeleen, we need to get out of here, don't we?'

'I suppose that's the plan,' she says in a sarcastic tone.

'Somehow we need to find our way out, but how? I'll have to think of something.'

'I'll stick by you; don't worry. I don't want to be alone here. I'm scared, you know,' she whispers.

I swear I'll protect her with my life. Nothing bad will happen to her as long as she sticks with me. I do hope we get out alive. I don't want to worry her too much; I have to make sure I lead the way. We'll head up the path I came from and down that path on the right. We'll likely find a lot of unknown creatures there, so we'll have to be careful.

She clutches on to me. 'I'm frightened, Mike.'

I feel her warmth as she snuggles up to me. I brush my fingers against her skin, gently. I need to make her feel protected. She seems fragile, and I have to make her my top priority. Losing her would be a shame; I can't bear the thought of being on my own again.

So far she seems to be quite a sweet person, and she seems to have a good heart. She's snuggled up to me, as if she's afraid I might disappear. I can feel her shaking. Maybe she needs to get used to the fact that she is not on her own anymore. I am very lucky and grateful she found me.

'Noeleen, we need to go.'

She smiles at me. 'Okay.'

CHAPTER 13

No Way Out

I pick up the notebook and place it in the side pocket of the backpack. *Won't be needing this anymore*, I think, *unless she wishes to read something from it.*

'If you get cold, you can have my jacket okay. Please don't be shy to ask for it.'

'Thanks, Michael. You are so kind.'

Her voice makes me feel like jelly inside. Every man should be a gentleman with any woman, no matter who she is. That's always been my belief. But unfortunately these days, not many men know how to treat a woman right. And the ones who do never get the chance to prove themselves, because they are put in the same category as all other men.

I stand up and bend down in front of her. I grab her hand to help her up. We are in no rush to get out of here. But we do need to head out of this cave. I try to think which way would be best. Shall we head back to the open field? Or the desert? Or maybe the other path? I think we need to make decisions as we go.

I take a quick glance at the end of the cave. I notice that my house door isn't there anymore. The back of the cave is composed of some kind of unknown substance, unlike the rest of the cave walls. Why my home was in this world is quite a mystery. I cannot figure it out. Maybe it's all planned out by someone and the pure purpose of me being here is the girl, Noeleen. What a beautiful name.

She is just staring at me. I don't look so good at the moment, and my clothes are rather messed up. A good suit gone to ruin here. The thought that she might have a slight attraction to me makes me feel volatile, as I'm not usually very good with women.

'Noeleen, wait here for a minute.'

'Where are you going?' I can hear fear in her voice.

'Don't worry. I'm not going far, just to the end of the cave. I need to investigate something.'

I smile at her to give her reassurance that she'll be okay. I walk slowly to where the door of my house was before. The cave, bar that area, hasn't changed. Where previously my front door was concealed behind thick vines, the strange substance, grey and wet to the touch has covered the back wall. I grab the penknife and scrape a bit off. As I scrape the grey substance, I reveal a sparkle.

I shout her name. '*Noeleen!*' The echo of my voice engulfs the cave.

'Mike?'

'Come have at look this.'

She rushes towards me. The creature seems to be sound asleep, and there is no need to get it up just yet.

'Woooooowwww,' she says. Her eyes widen, and she smiles. 'Mike, what is that?'

'I don't know. Let me scrape some more of this stuff off the wall.'

I use the penknife Noeleen found in the backpack earlier and scrape hard against the wall, removing the thick unknown substance from a large area of the wall and revealing what looks to me like diamonds. They look flawless – with no inclusions whatsoever. Thousands of them are clumped together behind the substance, forming a wall. I bash against it, but the surface of this wall is solid, and nothing happens. This cave is amazing. What seems to be gold covers the ground, red crystals are imbedded in places on the ceiling, and now this? It definitely doesn't resemble any of the caves I've seen back on earth. I've been to two different caves. One was made entirely of a hard rock like limestone, and the other was full of stalagmites and stalactites.

She talks as if this world is now her best friend. 'Are those diamonds?'

'I can't be sure, Noeleen. They certainly look like diamonds. They sparkle, and they would be worth a fortune back home, eh?'

'Do you think I could try and collect some?' she says, her interest clearly piqued. They do say diamonds are a woman's best friend.

'I've already tried bashing at the wall, but nothing came loose. Let me use the back end of the penknife. Maybe that will work.'

I hold on tightly to the handle of the penknife and strike the wall hard – as hard as I can. Nothing seems to happen. Uncontrollably, I bash at the wall until a little piece, no bigger than a thumbnail, falls to the floor. I kneel to pick it up. It's heavy, and it seems to be a perfectly shaped round diamond. The entire wall is like that; it's full of flawless stones of different shapes. But there are so many compacted together. I guess this explains why the wall is so solid.

I gently grab Noeleen's hand and place the diamond in her palm. She looks at me and *smiles*. *'Thank you, Mike.'*

'It's okay. I hope you like it. If that was a diamond, it would be worth quite a bit for sure. It's huge.'

'You got it for me. I would never sell it.'

She wouldn't sell it? Wow, how sweet. She keeps getting better and better. I obviously blush at her comment and say nothing more. I don't want to ruin this moment. Seeing her smile like this makes me feel a sense of happiness. Every time she smiles and looks me in the eye, my palms get sweaty, my heartbeat elevates, and I feel somewhat aroused.

I grin at her. 'What will you do with the stone then?'

'Well, I'll just look at it. I mean, wow. What is this place?'

She seems to have let go of all her fears of being here. This cave is a safe haven, but it's definitely a dead end and not a way out of this world. She holds her arm out and hands the stone to me.

'Could you hold it for me? I have no pockets in this dress and don't want to lose it once we get out of this cave.'

'Sure, I'll place it in the inside pocket. I've just remembered. Did you see that egg I had in the bag?'

'*Yes, I did*! What kind of creature do you think it belongs to?'

'Well, I found a clutch of those eggs under a rock in the ocean.'

'Isn't it weird that I haven't felt hungry at all since I've been here?' she says and laughs.

'That's true, eh. We can't delay any longer. We have to go. Top priority is to find our way out of this world.'

'Okay, Mike.'

I walk to the creature and stroke its head to wake it up. It opens its eyelids and stretches out.

Raaaarrrrrrrrrrrrrr.

It wags its tail from left to right, staring at me. I think it's excited to see that I'm awake. I'm glad it hasn't abandoned me. Without this little guy, I'm not sure what protection I would have against the beasts that live here.

I pat my thigh. 'Come on, boy.' The creature follows us as we walk out of the cave.

'Have you not given it a name, Mike?' she asks.

'Nope. Why don't you give it a name?' She takes a couple of seconds to think about it. 'Errrrrmmmm, Lido …. Yes, Lido.'

'Okay sounds good.'

I don't care what we call it, but Lido sounds good. And why not? I never thought about naming it. We both assume it's a male. But it could be a female.

We start moving towards the path she found me on. We walk past the lake. 'Good thing you found me, Noeleen,' I proclaim.

She nods. 'Yes it was, eh?'

We walk up the path, taking it slow, with Lido following on our trail. We don't really talk much while we walk. Noeleen seems tired, and we need to find somewhere to rest, as she didn't sleep at all while she was taking care of me. She lay down and nodded off for a few moments, but I wouldn't call that sleep. She must be quite knackered.

'Why don't we stay in the cave, Noeleen? We could just walk back. It's not that far.'

She looks at me, and I can see she agrees. We turn back and, feeling relaxed, we plod along back to the cave. I notice that the colour coming from the lake has changed.

'Wasn't that green earlier? I ask.

'Didn't really look.'

How can she not look? This place is amazing. 'Well, it's a red light shining out from it now, and it was definitely green before.'

'I was too busy saving you, remember?' She giggles, biting her bottom lip.

That's so hot. The lip biting needs to stop, unless she wants me to unleash my kinky side. It's the biggest turn -on for me. 'Yes, I remember. And thank you. I do appreciate it. Look at how beautiful that looks.'

'It does, doesn't it?'

We head towards the cave entrance, and as soon as we get inside, we both relax and take our time to unwind.

CHAPTER 14

Disorientated Beauty

As we rest, I can't stop looking at her. My god, she is absolutely gorgeous, like an angel fallen from heaven, here to see me – to protect me (although I'm the one who'll be doing the protection in this world).

She tends to smile at me a lot. She stares through my eyes and clutches onto my soul every time she gazes this way. She makes me feel nervous; my heart beats hard against the inside of my chest. I feel the chemicals rush through my body. And my palms are getting sweaty. She makes me feel amazing inside. She looks deep inside my mind, sensing my attraction towards her, preying on my weakness, and making herself highly appealing to me.

I can't find any flaws, although my eyes are locked with hers. I can't seem to gaze anywhere else. *Michael, smile back, mate,* I tell myself. *Say something.* I can't do anything about my inability to talk to her. I can't stop looking at her big brown eyes. I can't get enough of her breathtaking smile.

I want to get closer to her, I want to grab her arm and pull her towards me. I need to make that first move, show her that I'm her man. I'll kiss her soft red lips, hold her waist … Let it happen. *Do something.*

Baby, I want to kiss you so bad. But what if you turn me down? How do I know you want it as bad as I do? What if she doesn't? Why am I being hesitant? *Come closer, Noeleen. Make your move, Michael.* Let's face it. I can't do it just yet. I hardly know her, and she hasn't yet gotten to know me.

I look away for a while. But she just sits there. I wonder what she's thinking about so silently. What amazes me the most about her is how clean her skin looks. Her complexion is fair, and her skin smooth and free of blemishes or scars. Her eyebrows are sculpted to perfection, and she has no facial hair as far as I can see. She doesn't seem to have much make-up on.

I try to not look at her too much, but I tell you what, I could never have enough of her. Her body is great the way it is, and her face tops any beauty I've ever seen. Is she the girl of my dreams? I think so.

'Michael,' she says quietly

I stay silent for a while, and then, with a slight stutter, I answer, 'Yes, Noeleen?'

'Are you okay? You seem very silent.'

I smile at her and look down to the ground. 'Erm, yes I'm okay. Are you okay?'

'Well, yes, but you are keeping a distance it seems. Did I say something to offend you?'

'No, sweet Noeleen, just thinking. That's all. Give me some time to relax a bit.'

'Okay, me too. We both need to rest.'

Her voice sounds so amiable, and she's very sweet to talk to. Although I don't know her personality yet, she seems like quite a lovely person.

For a while, I keep looking at the ground, thinking of what might happen here. What if we are stuck in this world? I need to forget about this, so I look at her. She seems to be thinking about something. She's staring out into the distance. We're both sitting very close to the entrance of the cave. I notice her cute small nose. It has a slightly upward shape to it, and her puffy cheeks have a slight tinge of red. She's quite young, I'm guessing, as she has no wrinkles at all. I look at her pale skin, wondering if she likes getting tanned. I still have so much to learn about her.

Looking out myself, all I see is a white plain and the red tinge from the lake. The sun has actually changed its position, and I can see about three-quarters of it on the horizon. It's dark red at the bottom as it sets. The days here must be much longer than those on earth, as I have been here for a while already, and this is the first sunset I am witnessing. It's great timing now that she's here. Around the sun, the moons are no longer visible, and the sky seems slightly pink with a hint of red. The sunset here is beautiful. I take the opportunity to get closer to her.

'Noeleen, get over here. Let's watch the sunset together.'

She smiles, stands up, and walks towards me. She lies down in front of me with her back to my chest. 'Cuddle me, please,' she says with her soft sweet voice.

I wrap my arms around her, kissing her on the cheek. I definitely wouldn't imagine myself with anyone else watching this beautiful scene. Beats being at the cinema. This view is made for this moment with her. It feels like this world is made to bring us together. As long as she is safe, I'm happy, and I don't expect anything in return – not for now anyway. As much as she's enjoying her time with me, I'm still not so confident anything will happen between us. Some people are naturally too nice, and it seems like they're flirting when they're really not.

'Are you comfortable?'

'Yes,' I answer.

I couldn't think of a better way to spend the evening. Lying in front of me, she looks comfortable. I can smell her scent. Her hair smells fruity and it's soft against my face as I rest on her head.

She seems to be relaxing. She seems a perfect combination of loose and composed. She obviously feels safe in my arms. The sun goes down very slowly, so slow its movement is hardly noticeable, but the view can't be beaten. The path and the hedges obscure the sunset slightly, but that doesn't matter here.

She points into the distance. 'Wow, Mike. Look at that.'

'Yes, I've seen those creatures before.'

At last she has noticed something here – a flock of the majestic flying creatures gliding across the red plain. *One of those creatures killed Rickard, thank god they are not anywhere close to here.* Still, the perfect view and I'm sharing a perfect moment with a breathtaking gal. The creatures seem to be migrating somewhere, but I can't be sure. They leave a nice blue glow as they pass by.

'Michael.'

'Yes, Noeleen?'

'Are we safe here?'

'As long as we stick together, we will be absolutely fine. Don't forget; we have Lido with us. He has come in handy in the past.'

I can't tell her I'm not sure if we're safe. She already fears this place. I don't want to make it worse.

Lido seems to have taken a liking to Noeleen, as it curls up on her lap, purring like mad. I wish I had a camera with me. I've seen so many things I'd love to photograph. The sun edges downwards on the horizon behind the hedges and trees. Slowly, the sky grows dark, revealing a spectacular view of meteor showers. Hundreds of them bombard the atmosphere one after another, flying by swiftly through the heavens above, and then loads of tiny specs of light start to show high up in the cosmos – stars. It's not totally dark yet, so I wonder what the sky will look like once it's completely pitch-black. None of the moons are visible yet.

She turns her body around and faces me, holding herself up. 'Mike, do you mind if I lie down for a bit? I need to sleep.'

'Yes of course.'

I gently push her forward so I can get up, helping her stand in the process. We go deeper inside the cave. I grab my bag, sit down, and rest my back against the cave wall.

'Lay your head on my thighs and try and get some rest,' I suggest.

She gets down on the floor and lays her head on my lap.

I make a childish joke. 'Want me to read you a bedtime story?'

She giggles, but I'm not convinced I should have said that.

She smiles at me as I look down at her and shuts her eyelids.

'Sweet dreams, sweet Noeleen,' I whisper.

CHAPTER 15

Rest, Sweet Noeleen

I want to say things to her but I can't. She might think I'm moving too fast. But I've been spending time with her for a while, and the more I get to know her, the more I'm falling for her. Every time she talks to me, I feel a sense of security. I feel sad at the same time; I shouldn't be afraid to tell her how I feel. I know it's too early yet. I have to refrain from sharing my thoughts with her for a little bit longer. Patience is a virtue.

From what I've gathered, she doesn't trust easily. I need to tread very carefully if I'm to make this work. We get along well, and I find her attractive. The way she holds me and the way she looks at me is a very good sign, but are these things enough for me tell her how I feel?

I keep my thoughts to myself and gaze down at her as she sleeps. She looks comfortable, and I don't want to wake her from her dreams.

I stroke her head gently for a while, just gazing at the other side of the cave. I'm not really thinking about anything at this point. Feeling her breath and her warm body makes me feel addicted to her touch.

I close my eyes and contemplate life with this girl. She must be very popular judging by the way she looks. I can imagine that all day long random guys try their luck with her. They probably think she'll give them what they want. I bet she feels like she doesn't get respect from anyone. My best friend tells me loads of stories about how guys try getting with her, even when she's in a relationship. Why can't people respect that you're with someone and leave you alone? Why can't they let it be? She used to tell me how guys would constantly flirt with her and even ask her to meet up with them. I would hate to be a woman these days.

My aim with Noeleen is to show her that I'm not like any other guy. I actually have a lot more respect for her then she thinks. She doesn't realise it yet. And my biggest fear is that someone else will grasp her away from me before I get the chance to show her what respect means. We aren't going to be stuck in this world forever after all.

'You are so beautiful, Noeleen.' I say this in a gentle voice, more like a whisper.

She turns to her side, wrapping her right arm round my waist, and smiles. *Oh crap, I think she heard me. I don't think she is asleep.* I blush a little bit and start playing with her hair, brushing my fingers through it. Even though it's messed up and slightly knotted in some areas, it still feels very soft.

'Sleep, darling, I'm watching over you. No harm will come to you while I'm here.'

My creature, or Lido as she calls it, sleeps. Its tail is wrapped around its face, and I can see it breathing. It makes a slight grunting noise and is deep in sleep, I suspect.

I shut my eyes and try to sleep for a while. I can't sleep long, though; I need to watch over Noeleen and my creature. My eyelids are closed. I'm still wide awake though. I can hear her breathing, and she seems to be asleep now. She's so cute.

'Mmmmmm.'

Is she talking in her sleep?

'Where ...mmm.'

How sweet. She seems to be trying to say something, but I can't understand her mumbling.

I place my hand on her arm and stroke it gently. 'I'm still here, sweetheart,' I whisper so as not to wake her.

Yet again, I shut my eyes, still wary of what's going on around me, and I smile gracefully as she cuddles into me. I notice she has goosebumps all over her arms, I guess she's cold. I'm feeling quite warm myself, so I slowly edge forward so my back isn't resting against the wall, remove my suit jacket, and place it over her body. As the inside of the jacket is very warm, it should keep her warm.

As the firmament gets darker and darker, I notice that the cave wall is slightly lit – as if it's glowing in the dark. It looks absolutely magnificent. The light is reflecting from the walls to the red crystals affixed to the cave's ceiling. The crystals sparkle as the light shines through them. I feel safe and comfortable; the cave's walls feel rubbery. I wonder how long we'll have to wait till morning comes. *If the night is as long as the day time*, I contemplate ... 'Wow,' I whisper. That will be boring for me. I plan to watch over her and Lido. I can't sleep.

I reach into the backpack and pull it towards me to look at the contents. I haven't yet had a proper look.

Taking a quick peep inside, I notice the egg. It looks the same as before. I wonder what's inside it. Something magical, I'm sure. I take the egg out of the backpack and place it near me. I take another peep inside the bag. I find a torch, which I grab, and click the button to light it up. Great, it still works. I hold the egg in my right palm and flash the torchlight on it. I can actually see inside the egg, where there appears to be some kind of embryo. In fact, it looks like it could hatch anytime. I have no idea what it will be and wonder if it will survive as it's not in the ocean. I try to imagine what kind of fish or sea creature the little embryo will be. But it will have to remain a mystery until it hatches.

'Mmmmmm.'

I wonder what she's dreaming about. She seems comfortable and content, which is enough for me to keep me from worrying. I'm sure she would have woken up by now if she was having a nightmare.

I place the egg in the bag and rest for a while, patiently waiting for the sun to rise so we can get moving and get out of this cave. As much as I don't want to, I can't keep myself from keeping my eyes open.

I start feeling drowsy, but I'm so on edge I can't nap at all. *Sleep, Michael, I tell myself. Get some rest. You're safe in here.* As much as I would like to shut my eyes and sleep, I cannot trust this world. But I need to rest. I have to. The cave does not seem like a danger area, and we are totally safe.

Noeleen is safe and the creature is still fast asleep.

I feel myself start to doze off. My eyes are getting heavy. I shut my eyelids.

CHAPTER 16

My Street

The sound of a car horn wakes me up, and consternation quickly spreads over me.

Noeleen is still sleeping with her head on my thighs. Where are we?

Where's Lido?

I gently shake Noeleen's shoulder. 'Wake up,' I say softly.

She yawns and gradually opens her eyes. 'Mike …mmm.'

'We need to get up. We're not in the cave anymore,' I say, and I can hear the excitement in my voice.

'Where are we?' she asks, flustered.

'Looks like my street.'

I stand up, helping Noeleen to stand also. Near us, I see my road sign – Monrose Street. The road, which is old, is made of uneven, mostly cracked, grey bricks, and faded double yellow lines delineate the two lanes. The metal poles on which hang the street lights are rusted. Across the road, parked cars line up the one-way system.

I take a deep breath of fresh air. 'Ahhhhh, smells like home all right,' I note. The smell of baking bread drifts from the bakers up the road. The street lights are dimmed, as the sun hasn't yet risen. I look at my watch. It seems to be working, and the time is 6.21 a.m. I look up the street. A slight bit of fog quilts the road, and the cars appear wet, so I presume it's been raining.

I slide my fingers through the gaps in between her fingers. 'Let's go home, Noeleen.'

We walk along the pavement. To our right, several shops, all with their shutters closed – it's still too early for any of them to be open – line the road. The street is quite barren at this time.

I wink at her. 'Let's go to mine. Please don't look at the state of my place. It's not very nice. About four months ago, I entered into an agreement on this house, and the landlord said he'd sort out all the issues. Nothing has been done yet, and it's getting to a stage where I might have to get legal advice.'

'Is it that bad?' she asks.

'It's worse than bad. It's not really habitable at all.'

'Wow. But I'm not bothered what your place looks like, Mike. As long as I'm with you, I'm happy.'

She's too sweet. I'm very lucky to have met her. 'Thank you for being sweet. You are so lovely.'

She blushes and looks away. We walk at a slow steady pace, passing different coloured doors. I notice that people's bins seem full, which reminds me I need to take my rubbish out for the bin man to pick up. I miss it sometimes, but luckily I don't accumulate too much rubbish.

'This street is very tranquil – so quiet and empty.'

She's right. Everyone is peaceful and relaxed here. At this time in the morning, people are either asleep or at work. Charlotte, who works in the bakery, is a nice girl. She always makes me a mean sandwich.

'My house isn't too far,' I assure her. 'Are you hungry at all, Noeleen?'

'Not really.'

My stomach grumbles. 'I'm a little peckish'

I slide my hand in my right pocket and grab my keys. Holding them, I think, *Yes, I'm home.* It's nothing special, but it's better than a cave.

'Hey, Noeleen.'

'Yes?'

'I just want to warn you now. The cave is much better than my house.'

She laughs. 'Oh well.'

Okay, so that's out of the way. She knows about my house. I feel slightly reluctant taking her here, but there's nothing I can do about it now.

'This is my door. I apologise in advance.' The paint on the door is peeling off. Cobwebs full of deceased arachnids cover each top corner of the door. The frame is damaged and full of cracks, creating a great habitat for all types of insects.

I slide my key into the keyhole and turn it right. The mechanism of the lock makes a distinct clicking sound, and I push the door open.

'Home at last.' For once, I'm smiling here.

I walk straight into the kitchen, light up the gas hob, grab a saucepan, and fill it up with water. 'First things first.' I get the last two eggs out of the fridge and place them in the saucepan. I have nothing else. That will do.

'Noeleen, come over here. Make yourself at home sweetheart.'

She walks over to me and pushes me against the cupboard.

'Mmmmm, Noeleen.'

I pull her closer, so she is pressed against my body.

'I can feel your heartbeat,' she says, pressing her palm against my chest.

I place my right hand on the side of her face and brush my fingers through her hair while looking her deep into her eyes. I lean forward, and our lips lock. My eyes are closed, and neither of us seems to want to pull away.

The kiss feels amazing. I can feel her lips against mine. I bite her lower lip and brush my tongue against it. Her lips feel delicate against my tongue. I breathe heavily as she pulls me closer to her, brushing her fingers through my hair. I kiss her slowly; this is definitely what a passionate kiss should feel like.

I open my eyes for a split second and pull away, just to get a chance to gaze into her eyes. I kiss her again, hard, and our lips are moving faster now. I feel her tongue pressing against mine. She compels me, and I'm sexually aroused. My right hand massages her lower back, and my left is on the side of her neck. I can hear her breath. She must be really enjoying this. I could just rip her clothes off right here. She is so hot.

The sound of the water boiling over reminds me that I'm boiling eggs. I stop kissing her and turn the knob to turn the flame off. I strain the water and attempt to peel the eggshells into the sink.

She looks at me with a frown. 'Seriously, Mike?'

I poke my tongue at her. 'What? Can't waste the eggs. I'm starving anyway.' I move close to her, kiss her on the cheek, and go back to peeling the second egg.

She laughs. 'I guess I have no choice here, eh, Mike.'

I quickly eat the eggs and put my attention back on her. She just stands there, her arms crossed, looking around. She's probably thinking about how bad my place looks or wondering how I can live in a place that's in such disrepair. She looks bored and in need of my attention. Moving close to her, I grab both her arms, wrap them around me, and give her a peck on the lips. She pulls away and smiles at me.

She holds her nose and sticks her tongue out at me. 'Have a drink, Mike. I smell eggs.'

'I am sure it's not that bad ... Is it?' I'm flustered, and I feel myself blushing.

'Get a drink,' she whispers, winking at me.

What an embarrassing moment. I walk over to the end of the kitchen, open the cupboard door, and grab a glass. It looks slightly dusty, so I rinse it under the tap and fill it up. I down the water as fast as possible, not to waste any time. 'Where were we, gorgeous?'

I give her a peck on the lips.

'Better now?' I say.

She winks at me yet again. 'Yes, a little better.'

She grabs my tie and pulls me close to her. I place my left hand on her hip and caress the side of her neck with my right arm and edge forward to kiss her again. She turns her face sideways as I go in to kiss her and whispers in my ear, 'Shall we take it upstairs?'

I take a hold of her arm. 'Mmmm, Noeleen .... Let's go.'

We both walk out of the kitchen and run up the stairs. I stop on the way up and start kissing her. I unzip her dress, and as I'm doing so, she starts to unbuckle my belt. 'Take me to your bedroom, Mike,' she says.

Without hesitation, I lift her and carry her to my bedroom. I set her down and pull her close to me, kissing her lips passionately. I slide the straps of her dress down her arm and slide it off her. In the heat of the moment, she takes my suit jacket off and rips my shirt open. She must be feeling quite hot, as she pulls my unbuckled belt and throws it behind her. She unbuttons my trousers and pulls them down.

I push her onto the bed and get on top of her, rubbing myself hard against her and kissing her neck and body.

Eager to go to the next step, she says, 'I want you inside me, Mike.'

I look up at her as I'm kissing the inside of her thighs. 'I'm going to tease you for a while.'

She grabs a handful of my hair. 'Mmmm. Michael, I'm so hot for you right now.' She is definitely enjoying my tongue rubbing and caressing her genital area. She moans as I slide my fingers inside her.

She can't seem to resist. 'Mike, I want you so bad. Come up here.'

I gaze straight up at her and slide both my hands up her body and grope her breasts. I play with her nipples as I push my tongue along her sensitive genital area.

She starts raising her voice at me as she moans. 'Mike, I want you. Don't tease me like this any longer.'

As much as I am enjoying this, I give in and make love to her as if I have never made love to any other woman before.

We both just lay in bed, sweating and breathing hard.

That was amazing. Her head rests on my chest, and her naked body presses against mine. Her eyes are closed, revealing her smudged, dark purple eye shadow. And her warm body is perfect – not even a single flaw. Her curves are ideal, the kind that would make any man go crazy. Perfect.

'I'm not finished yet,' I whisper, rubbing my tongue gently against her sensitive earlobe.

She looks straight at me, smiles, and starts kissing me again. 'I'm tired. You have completely taken my breath away.'

I lay on the bed. Noeleen is holding on to me, comfortable and completely knackered. I grab the quilt cover and slide it over us.

With confidence I say, 'Come here, gorgeous.'

She comes closer, lying face down with her chest on my body, looking at me. I wonder what she's thinking.

'You are amazing, Mike.'

'How am I?' I say.

She winks at me. 'I think you know.'

Damn right I know. She can hardly move; I gave her a good performance back there.

'Come on top of me.'

'Mmm, Michael.'

I pull her over me and kiss her slowly while scratching her back hard.

Eventually we fall asleep, all cuddled up.

CHAPTER 17

Back Again!

I wake up before her, startled and confused.

'Mmm.'

Where are we? I look around and see what appear to be cacti hanging from the ceiling of a different cave. I'm lying on the ground, which feels like a material I've never before come across – like grass but much softer. My body seems to have sunken in a little, and a mould has been created around me and Noeleen. The creature lies there sleeping, its tail around its face covering its eyes.

I don't wake Noeleen, as she's lying with her head on my chest and her right arm around my waist. Her right leg is over mine, and she seems to be comfortably snuggled up to me. She breathes slowly, and she seems very relaxed.

As I look around, I notice light pouring in from the entrance of this cave. Loud noises from outside echo around the cavern. We seem to be in an open area in here, and water is flowing down one of the cave's walls, making a gurgling noise and trickling into a puddle that's nearly the size of a small pond.

On the other side, I can't see much through the darkness, but I make out a dark rocky substance.

I gently nudge Noeleen awake. Her beautiful waking noises echo around us.

'Mike? Where? Where are we?' she stutters.

'We are in some different cave I'm sure – completely different from the other cave. Look at the water streaming down the wall! That wasn't there before.'

'Yes, we must be in a different cave then,' she says quietly.

I explain as best I can that I haven't been outside this cave, so I can't be sure where we are. Half an hour ago, she was butt naked, cuddled up to me, and now she is dressed, and we are not on my bed anymore. I wonder what is going on here. This is a freaky situation.

I get up from the floor and kneel down to look for the torch in the backpack. I stand and start exploring the dark area of the cave to my right. The wall, which is solid and smooth, feels slightly rippled in some areas. I point the torch at the wall, and the light reflects back slightly, confirming that it has a glossy finish. It reminds me of dry lava rock back home. I reach for my keys and scrape some of the rock off the wall; it breaks off with ease. I flash the torch at the exposed rock and see what looks like some kind of red metal.

I scratch hard against this mysterious material. Wow. A beautiful red spark ignites. Once again, I flash my torch at the metal. Not so much as a mark reveals my tampering. I tap at it with the key, and it makes a clanging sound – more like ticking, like hitting the end of a key on a metal surface. But every time the metal part of my key hits the cave wall, a red spark is created. I shine the torch around the cave for a split second, revealing the intense blackness of the surrounding wall. This is really intriguing me, and I feel like a child with a new toy.

Using my key as a chisel, I start scraping off bits of the black substance, revealing more of the red metal.

'Michael? What are you doing over there?'

Grinning to myself, I answer, 'Nothing!'

I ignore her and continue to chisel the rock from the surface of the cave wall. Now and again, I flash the torch at it. Apparently, there's a lot of this metal, and curiosity keeps me at it for a while. Maybe I hope to unfold some kind of mystery in this cave – perhaps some kind of clue about how to get out of this world. I imagine unfolding a clue that will show me a way out or a way to become a better person in a better life. This is just a wall. But who knows? Nothing is unexpected in this world.

'Noeleen.' My voice bounces off the walls of the cave, echoing all over the place.

'Yes?'

Actually, she won't be interested in touching or knowing about the cave wall, so I don't say much about it. She should see this, though. Maybe she will be interested after all. It's not like this is normal on earth. This metal is flawless – it's so sleek, and not one scratch is on it. It has a kind of mirror finish to it, and I can vaguely see myself. I see that my trousers are torn at the knees. There isn't much light in here, so can barely make out what I look like. Flashing the light at the metal doesn't help; it just reflects back at me, blinding my vision slightly.

'Noeleen, can you come hold the flashlight for me, please?'

'Yes, sure.' She gets up and walks towards me, her footsteps echoing as she treads on the ground. I hand her the flashlight.

'Could you point it towards the wall, please?'

'Oh, Mike, let's go. I'm getting extremely bored.'

'Come on, sweetheart. Be patient. It's not like we have something to do here.'

I really don't know what to say to her; she just wants to leave. But why? It's not like we have some kind of plan. I don't know what she has on her mind, but I have nothing planned.

'If you want, you can go sit next to Lido while I explore'

She doesn't seem to be interested in joining my investigation. 'Okay then.'

I decide to go deeper into the cave. Using the flashlight to light up the way ahead, I walk at a slow pace, flashing the light from side to side and onto the ground. The cave floor is hardening as I creep into the darker area and it feels slightly slippery, as if oil has been spilt. I kneel down and scrape my fingers across the floor. 'Hmm,' I mutter. 'Seems to be some kind of grease.' I smell it and rub my fingers together. The thick grease smells nice. Very strange. Pointing the light at the grease, I see it's greenish layer covering what seems to be normal rock.

I decide to go back to Noeleen, as I can imagine she's pretty bored by now.

'You okay, sweetheart?' I ask.

'Yes, but I'm bored.'

'Okay, we need to get out of this cave and see what's going on here.'

She stands up, nudging Lido to wake up as she does so, and she walks over to me. I point the torch at her.

'Mike, get that out of my face.'

I let out a nervous laugh.'Can't see you otherwise.'

'Nothing to see here.'

I can actually imagine her face even in the dark – can imagine her smiling at me with those big brown eyes of hers and those cute cheeks. I wonder what's outside the cave. I'm not really afraid; I'm just speculating what to do next. I wish this world existed for real. I'm no longer sure what's real at the moment. I walk towards the lit area; the way out is clear and I feel intrigued and curious. I hope it's not another ocean; I don't want to get wet again.

As we are walking out, I start noticing that the cave is the same as before. Even the scratch marks I made on the ground are still there. Now, I'm confused. 'Noeleen.' I say slowly, 'we are still in the same place as before after all.' I point to the marks on the cave floor.

Her gaze follows my finger and when she sees it too, she draws her breath in sharply. 'Oh this place is a puzzle.' For a moment, she looks dazzled, and then her face drops. 'What do we do now?'

'Nothing to do but walk and explore,' I say, sounding more sure than I actually feel. 'It's kind of getting boring to me now though.'

Her tone turning sad, she replies, 'I'm tired of not knowing what's going to happen next.'

I stop and face her. Smiling at her, I decide to act silly; maybe that'll help her relax a little. I poke my tongue out at her and squint.

'He he, Mike, you are being silly. But it's making me laugh.' She giggles.

At least my silliness wasn't in vain. 'That's the idea. I hate to see you sad or worried. I know this place is an absolute mystery. But that's the way it is, and we have to find a way out. There is always a way out, as long as we don't get killed.' I laugh and place my hand on her shoulder. 'I'm not saying we're going to die. I am very positive and don't forget Lido. He has saved me a couple of times, and he's pretty cute too. Come here, boy.'

I slap my leg and whistle at the same time. Lido runs over on all fours. My creature rubs his head against the side of my leg and purrs at the same time. His colouration is vivid, and the contrast between the colours is striking. He's such a gentle creature, yet I know he can be aggressive.

'Let's get out of here, Noeleen.'

I peek out of the cave to make sure it's safe to leave. Everything seems quite the same as before. The thick snow and our footsteps and trail, along with the carcass of the fish Lido caught, are still there. The lake steams. I look up. A few clouds blanket the reddish purple sky, and the sun is glowing red high up. What a tranquil sight. Two of the moons are visible, one to the right of the sun. The other isn't far from it but seems higher.

I help Noeleen out of the tight entrance of the cave and walk towards the lake. She follows, and Lido seems to opt for a little exercise. He dives into the lake and comes back out, crawling onto the edge of the lake.

'Mike, I feel slightly thirsty,' Noeleen says. 'I think there was a bottle of water in the bag.'

I remove a strap from my shoulder, shuffle the bag to my front, unzip the top, and put my arm inside to have a feel around.

'Ahhh, I think you're right.'

I take out a bottle full of liquid, unscrew the top, and hand it to her.

She giggles. 'I won't drink it all.'

'Thank you.'

She takes a few sips of the water and hands the bottle back to me with the top unscrewed. After taking a few sips myself, I place the half-full bottle back in the pack. I pull the strap back up onto my shoulder, and we move on. I'm not too worried about Lido running away, so I leave him to swim and have a little run round the place.

We walk close to the lake and look down, trying to determine its depths. Violent air bubbles blind our view of the lake bed, but we can still see the slight green luminescence coming from the plants that live deep within the lake, and it's a fascinating phenomenon.

We look at one another, as if we can read each other's minds, and then both start speaking at the same time.

'Shall we—'

I stop, and we both laugh. It seems we wanted to say the same thing.

'Go on, Mike. What where you going to say?'

'I was just going to suggest that we start heading towards the path and get out of here?'

She nods. 'Yep, exactly what I was going to say.'

CHAPTER 18

Do Not Let Go of My Hand, My Lovely!

I grab Noeleen's hand and nudge her towards me. Together, we set off towards the path, the creature following. It seems as though the hedges on either side of the path have been trimmed; cut leaves lie in piles on the ground.

'Are you noticing something different?' I ask.

'Erm, not really, other than the cut leaves.'

'They weren't here before,' I point out.

'I know, right? Someone else must be lurking around here.'

She's correct. We have to be very vigilant, and we need to keep our eyes peeled. I try not to think too much about this as we walk up the path. I have to give the unknown groundskeepers credit. They've done a great job on the trim of the hedges – an exceptional job.

It's not long before we're back at the spot where the path splits. It seems our next approach should be to take the other path. But first, I decide to go back to the open field to get the briefcase. It's sad that I have to walk past Rick's corpse again.

'We need to get the briefcase,' I say.

'Okay, why are we going back there?' she asks.

'To look for clues, eh.'

She has to ask so many questions. I don't blame her, but I find some of the questions she comes up with difficult, as I can't really be sure of the answer so don't know what to say. And I don't want to lie to her about anything. The last thing I want is to get a bad name with her. She seems curious, yet she asks because she wants to get out of here. But she must realise that being here is also difficult for me. She sits down on the rock, where the split in the path lies.

'This is comfy. It's a rock though ….Why?'

'Yes, it's definitely comfortable,' I agree. 'I sat on that rock for quite a while. Just gaze down on both paths and enjoy the tranquil view.'

She yawns. No way she's already tired.

'Ohhhh, Michael. I'm going to fall asleep here.'

I walk over, grab her arm, and pull her up. I can't let her get too comfortable here, or we'll end up wasting our time in this same area.

'Ahhhhh, let me relax.'

'But we need to keep moving,' I say, sounding a bit stern. I can't be too soft. This place isn't the safest of all the places I've been. She has to understand this.

'We will get time to relax, don't worry sweetheart' I say.

We start moving again, and Lido stumps along with us, not a care in the world. Maybe my creature doesn't care where we're heading.

Before too long, we'll get to where we have to turn right into the woodland area. The path itself hasn't changed much. Other than some dead leaves on the ground, it looks the same.

The opening into the woodland is exactly the same, as well, so I have no problem determining which way to go.

We turn right and start walking through the woodlands.

She points at one of the trees. 'There was an engraving on one of these trees,' she says.

'Really? I didn't notice anything when I was coming through here last time,' I reply.

'Did you engrave it yourself?' she asks

'Definitely wasn't me. Could have been Rick before he got attacked or whoever trimmed the hedges.'

'Oh, Mike, I'm so afraid. I'm so glad I met you here.'

'Thanks again for not leaving my side, Noeleen.' I smile at her.

Looking confused, she replies, 'No problem, but I swear there was an engraving on one of these trees, and we have definitely gone past it.'

I've nearly gotten used to the fact that this place has magical properties, and nothing is unexpected here.

As we walk, I notice Rick's body still lies where I left it – untouched, the colourful leaves still adorning his chest and the moss still cradling his head.

'He seemed like such a nice guy, and I did try to save him,' I say quietly, 'but it was no good. He died in my arms. He looks like he's in peace. He did suffer, though.'

'What happened?' she asks.

'Well he got attacked by a creature, and I saved him. But I couldn't do enough to keep him alive. I paid my respects. He's the one that gave me the backpack. He said it would come in handy sometime. And it has so far. The notebook is hard to explain though. I never came across it until you read from it.'

We stand there over his body, paying our respects to what seemed like a great man.

'Give me a few minutes, Noeleen.'

'Take your time,' she says.

I take some time to think. On one knee, I put my head down and say a little prayer, hoping that Rick's soul is resting in peace. I wipe my face, as I feel quite emotional and a teardrop has trickled down my cheek. I still feel badly that I couldn't keep him alive.

After a few minutes, I decide we'd better get going. Noeleen just stands there holding Lido in her arms. Lido seems comfortable.

'How long have you been holding him for?'

'Not that long. He's quite happy. Shall we get going?' she says in her sweet girly voice.

'Come on, let's go. Actually, you wait here for a couple of minutes. I need to make sure its safe first.'

I walk over to the opening that leads to the field, looking in both directions, then and up to the skies. I don't see anything.

'Noeleen, you can come now, sweetheart.'

She walks over to me, and we look around for my briefcase. Both it and the notes seem to have disappeared.

'This is where I started my journey,' she explains.

'This is where I saved Rick. The mark in the forest floor from me dragging his body is still here.'

'Yes, that's what I followed to get to you,' she says. 'Good thing you left me clues to find you because I would have probably gone the wrong way.'

'I am glad you found me.'

'Let's walk around the edge of the field and see if we find some kind of opening that will lead beyond the field.'

'Yeah, okay.'

I hold her hand, and we walk across to where bushes surround the outskirts of the field. We look around for a gap. Maybe there is no way out of this field, other than the way we came from.

We've been walking for a while when, out of nowhere, a flash of black above my head catches my eye and something large throws me to the ground from behind, pushing me face forward into the earth. From the snarling sounds and what I can glimpse as I struggle to my knees, trying to throw my attacker off me, I guess it's one of those wolf-like creatures.

'Mike!'

'Noeleen,' I manage to shout. 'Run towards Rick's body and wait there. Ahhh, get off me!'

'I'm not going anywhere.'

Another of the creatures jumps out of the hedge and growls at Noeleen. The wolf-type creature stands in an intimidating position. Lido runs at the wolfish creature from its side and sinks its teeth into the beast. It howls as the poison kicks in and tumbles straight to the ground. I'm still struggling with the creature on my back, attempting to pull its leg downwards.

Lido hisses wildly at the creature. He looks ready to pounce, and I hope he'll kill it. The creature's claws are digging into the side of my arm.

As the pain kicks in, I feel my arm bleeding and fall onto my back, forcing the creature off me. Lido doesn't give it a chance to escape. He growls and snarls menacingly, ready to sink his teeth into the creature and inject his lethal venom into its veins.

'Come here, Noeleen. I need you to be close to me.'

She runs over, clutching onto my arms.

'I'm sorry I didn't listen to you and run, but I froze. I thought I was going to die.' She explains.

'Don't worry. You don't have to be sorry. At least you can see Lido in action now.'

Hsssssssss. Hsssssssssss.

The wolfish beast doesn't seem to be backing down, and Lido seems to be left with a situation. He looks ready to attack, but this time, the beast is facing him and ready to retaliate. Lido displays his crest and hisses wildly to intimidate it. At first, the wolf-like creature doesn't seem to feel threatened, but as Lido moves towards it, it takes a few steps back.

Eventually Lido makes a run towards the creature. Finally, it backs down and flees into the bushes.

Noeleen trembles with fear. 'Wow, Mike, I was so scared.'

'I know. Me too, sweetheart. Let's hope that doesn't happen again. Thanks to Lido, we're still alive.'

I take a closer look at the dead wolfish creature and examine it for a while. Its mouth is wide open, and the eyelids are shut. The wound where Lido bit the creature is inflamed and bleeding heavily.

'Come, sweetheart. Let's put this event behind us. You don't need to be afraid anymore.'

We keep walking and eventually find a hidden path. So we decide to walk through it. It's rough and full of stones and pebbles, and for the most part, the same trees we've encountered before line either side of the path, though a few patches of rocky terrain surround the area. Squawking noises keep me aware and cautious of this place.

We soon forget about the incident where we nearly got killed, and Lido seems as energetic as ever.

Noeleen and I hold hands as we walk along, jokingly betting about how we're getting out of here.

I poke my tongue out at her. 'You're going to owe me a lot of money if we keep making bets like this.'

She giggles and sticks her tongue out at me. 'No way.'

'Don't you think it's weird how we both ended here?'

'Yes, Mike' She squeezes my hand hard. 'Faith.'

I push her gently in a flirty way. She obviously knows I'm flirting. She does the same back, suggesting she's flirting back. How cute.

'Look to the distance, Noeleen.'

'What am I looking at?' she says in a cute kind of voice.

'Seriously, hon?' In the distance, I see a huge rocky area, as if we're walking towards a cliff that's not quite visible just yet. 'Haven't you noticed anything while you've been here?'

'Well, yeah, I have. But I'm not very into this world. It's scary for me.'

'Aww, sweet, don't be afraid. I'm here, remember?' I pull her over so she's in front of me, wrapping both my arms round her.

'Mike, thank you. Sometimes I want to believe you're real.'

What does she mean by that? She can feel my chest moving as I breathe. 'What do you mean, hon?'

'Well, I've been used by every guy I've ever met. I've been treated like muck. Three different guys cheated on me, and one guy even got married to someone else while he was with me. Another lied about everything just to keep me sweet. Then you come along. You don't expect anything. You treat me like I'm some princess; you are kind and gentle. What can I say? Guys like you don't exist, eh!'

'Sorry' I smile. 'I don't want to be like all the other guys. I've been through a lot as well. I understand where you're coming from. We should take things slow and keep it relaxed.'

She backs away from the hug, smiling and giggling. 'You see what I mean? Mike, you are so sweet.'

'Noeleen, let's keep moving,' I assert.

'Okay.' She grabs my hand as we start moving. Not much is here, so we just keep walking on the rugged terrain of the path, surrounded by trees and mostly grassland.

'I'm so tired of walking, Mike. When will we get out of here?'

'I don't know, but it's best we keep moving. Just enjoy the gorgeous views and don't think about it.' I'm trying to stay positive and constantly reassure her that nothing is wrong with this place. Deep down, I have no idea what's happening, but I'm keeping a straight face, as I don't want her to panic or feel afraid.

As we move closer to the cliff, the spectacular view wows me. I hold my arm out in front of her to hold her back. It's quite a large drop. I doubt we'd survive a fall. In the distance, I see a very small island, surrounded by tall cliffs. Only it's tiny – we could walk around it in less than twenty minutes – and doesn't seem habitable. The sea crashes against the cliff walls around the island. Boulders and loose rocks surround its edges. It seems desolate and hard to get to, even by boat. The shallow seas around it would make it hard for any boat to find a safe place to land.

I look beyond the island. Dark blue clouds blanket the red sky. A couple of the moons are visible, as a patch of the sky is clear of clouds. Rustling through my backpack, I find a set of binoculars. I see a few of those flying creatures swarming the island. There's no mistaking their beautiful colouration. These creatures are truly majestic, and I enjoy this opportunity to see them up close. Their heads are purple and dotted with tiny red spots. Teeth protrude from their lower jaw, and the bone on top of their eyes seems to be a bulge – for protection I presume. The top of their head are covered with numerous large feathers that extend to the middle of their backs and flow in the wind as they fly gracefully around the island.

I pass the binoculars to Noeleen. 'Have a look,' I say, smiling at her, amazed by those majestic creatures.

'Okay.' She takes them and stares at the creatures for a few minutes. 'Mike, wow; they are really nice.'

She doesn't sound enthusiastic, but at least she has had a look.

'Let's go back,' I say. 'There's nowhere else to go.'

'Mike, why don't we sit here for a while,' she suggests.

'Yeah sure, no problem.'

CHAPTER 19

Get to Know Me

We both sit down on the edge of the cliff. She places her left hand on my lap and kisses my cheek.

She giggles and whispers, 'I'm such a romantic, aren't I, nugget?'

She called me nugget. I try to hold back from laughing out loud.

I laugh.

'What are you laughing at?'

'Well, your fault. You called me a nugget.' I squeeze her arm gently and laugh once again. 'And yes, you are being romantic, aren't you?'

'I wouldn't say I'm a romantic kind of gal, Mike.' She blushes.

'What would you say then?'

'I don't know, but I'm definitely not a romantic. Can you cook?'

Wow she changed the subject there. I think I'm embarrassing her a little. With a smile on my face, I answer, 'Yes, but of course. Can you cook?'

'Not really. I don`t need to.'

I nudge her gently. 'Why's that then, eh?'

'Well, you know, I live with my parents, and they cook for me.'

'What's your favourite dish then?'

'I like everything to be honest,' she says.

'Great. How about I cook you chicken with mushroom sauce at some point?' I can just imagine cooking for her in my grotty flat. Thinking about it, I realise it's a bad idea; I might give her food poisoning or something. I can hardly cook for myself there. 'On second thought, it's not really a good idea to cook for you.'

She looks at me and frowns. 'Why not? Why can't you cook for me? I was going to say that I love that dish before you changed your mind.'

I push her gently with my shoulder. 'Come on. Don't be sad. You've seen the state of my flat. It's horrendous.'

'Yes, okay, you have a point. But you know I don't mind your flat.'

'What is there to like about it?' I ask, curious.

'Okay, maybe it's not the best-looking flat, but we had a good time in there, didn't we?'

'That we did, but come on; you can't say it's not the best. You should say it's disgusting.'

'You think too much, Mike.'

Maybe I do think too much. I mean she actually sticks with me, even though my flat looks like a tip. Isn't she the perfect woman to have? She just seems a bit too good to be true, like most things that make you happy in life. They start off wonderful, and then they end up becoming a nightmare after a while. Noeleen seems different from any of my ex-girlfriends. My ex was so needy. It was constantly, 'Mike, get me this,' and 'Mike, I need that.' If I didn't tell her that I loved her a million times a day, she would accuse me of cheating. But she'd started off all nice and kind. Then she'd turned into an absolute nightmare after five months. I couldn't cope with her demands but was in love with her by then.

'Mike?' She pokes me to get my attention.

'Oh, hi.'

'You went all silent then. Are you okay?' she asks, her pitch higher than normal, suggesting she's worried.

'Yeah, yeah. I'm fine. I was just thinking about finding a way to cook for you in a clean environment.'

'Still worried about that?'

'Yes of course I am. I know you don't mind me cooking for you at my place. But at the end of the day, if I don't feel comfortable in that skanky flat, how can I feel comfortable cooking for you there. I mean, are you blind? How didn't you notice the way it looked and how bad it was in there?'

She smiles at me. 'Who said I was looking at the flat, eh?'

'Oh, what where you looking at then?'

'You of course.'

What is her issue, looking at me? I'm not sure what to think here. There's nothing to see. I'm just a normal depressed broke guy with no life living in a horrible flat. But then again, she isn't the same as anyone I've ever been with before. Not to mention her beauty. Her personality shines on me like the rays of the sun on a scorching summer day. I have to stop thinking negatively about the way she looks at me, the way she kisses my lips, and the way she tries to make me happy.

Maybe she has come into my life to change all that. I haven't felt depressed since she's been with me. And I've never felt like this before. She gives me a smile and keeps me on my toes.

We gaze into the distance, both agreeing on how spectacular the view is. It's such a beautiful view, with so much splendour.

Eventually I decide we have to get moving, as this is a dead end.

I take one last good look at the view in front of me and stand up. Grabbing her hand, I help her up, making sure she does not trip or slip.

'We need to head back,' I say.

'Where should we go next, Mike?'

'Did you go to the top of the path? That's where I started,' I tell her.

'Is that where there is a deserted area? And a lake with black water?'

'Yes,' I say.

'Yeah, we should check it out. That's where you started. I'm sure you said that, right?'

'I did, yes, and maybe where I started is the way out of here. We'll never know until we get there.'

We start moving towards the open field, again seeing nothing different from what we've seen before.

'Stop for a minute, Noeleen.'

'What's up?'

'I have a stone in my shoe, and it's bothering me,' I explain.

'Okay, sort it out then.'

I sit down on the hard ground and undo my laces. I then remove my shoe and tap it down to get the stone out.

'Much better; quite a big stone that was. Can't walk with stones in my shoe – too uncomfortable,' I say.

I get back up and hold her hand, and we start moving again; we're constantly moving. Deep inside my mind, I'm screaming, *Get me out of here.* And I'm sure Noeleen is feeling the same way. The sky makes me feel a bit drowsy, especially if I look at the sun for too long and those beautiful moons that are constantly in view.

Eventually, we get to the open field. The dead wolfish creature is still lying there, although there's evidence of some movement near it.

'Do you see that, Noeleen?' I point towards the dead carcass of the wolf and explain that something's moving near it.

'Yes, actually. Are we going to check it out?'

'Yep. You know me. I'm curious, and I need to know what that movement is.'

We cautiously move closer to it, me holding Lido in my arms; I don't want it to attack whatever it is.

From the way the creature is moving, I guess it's a baby wolf creature. It's tiny, and it's hanging around near what I guess is the mother making squeaky noises. The wolf creature must have been pregnant. I'm surprised the venom didn't kill the baby also.

I feel quite sorry, as the baby won't survive on its own, and I hope another creature will come and raise it. The little baby is black, and its eyelids are closed. It doesn't really do much and will die sooner or later.

'What are we going to do, Mike?'

'Nothing we can do here. We can't keep it,' I explain.

'Why don't you let Lido kill it?'

'Would end its suffering then I suppose. But what if another of it's kind comes to save it and finds it dead?' I say.

'Well I don't know. I feel like I'm going to cry. I feel so sorry for it. Can we go please?'

Wow, she is sensitive. Earlier these creatures nearly killed us, and now she's crying over a one of their babies. She amazes me with the stuff she comes out with sometimes. 'Okay then, let's move out.'

She probably thinks I'm being really insensitive at the moment. But what does she want me to do? If we stick around here for too long, more of those wolfish things will come and attack us, and we can't risk our lives like that again. This place seems like a hotspot for trouble.

We get going moving towards the opening in the trees where Rick's body lies. I'm thinking, *Safe zone at last.* Noeleen's still sobbing over the baby wolf creature, and that makes me sad. But she has to get over it sooner or later.

'Did you know Rick?' she randomly asks as we walk past him

'No. I just met him here.'

'Oh, I thought you knew him from the way you spoke about him.'

'No, no, but I could imagine myself being really good friends with him.'

As we walk, I notice a message engraved on a tree.

'Mike, look over there. That tree has a message on it. I think it's the same tree that had the engraving before, telling me to turn left.'

I place my hand on my face and drag it down with frustration. The engraving says, 'You are stuck here forever.' That message must be wrong. There's no way we can be stuck here forever. I really hope not anyway. I start to feel panicky and annoyed. That message could mean there's no way out of here. The question is, how did that message get there in the first place? Who engraved it?

I take a closer look, following the engraving with my index finger. The engraving is perfectly carved in the tree. And it smells quite bad, as some of the sap from the tree oozes out of the carved letters. I avoid touching the sap with my finger. I examine the words closely, I trying to figure out how it's been engraved. On the ground near the tree's base, bits of bark are scattered – the remains of the engraving. I kneel over to pick a piece up, holding my nose, as the smell is intense and disgusting.

'Michael.'

I stand and turn around to face her, as she is waiting for me to finish my little investigation. 'What's up, Noeleen?'

'Have you found any clues as to what whoever wrote that used to engrave this message and, more importantly, who engraved it?'

'I have no idea to be honest, but it looks like they used a corer of some sort, as the lettering is rounded and the remains lie on the ground at the base of the tree. This is no coincidence; someone else must be here. The hedges are trimmed, the path is man-made, and the briefcase has disappeared. I can't explain any of this, and the more I look at this engraving, the more frustrated I'm feeling.'

'Why don't we keep moving?' she suggests.

I think that would be best; I'm getting too wound up here, and regardless of what this note says, we can't give up all hope and be stuck in this strange world.

I walk towards Noeleen, and we start moving again towards the main path – trying to forget about the engraving on the tree.

'What's your favourite fruit?' I ask.

'Random question, but mango. What about yours?' she answers.

'My favourite fruit are nectarines.'

'I like them too, but they're quite messy. I don't like them when they're ripe. I prefer them crunchy,' she says.

'Me *too*,' I agree.

Ah, we have something in common, and that makes me feel happy. But the message that there is no way out makes me feel sick to my stomach.

We get to the opening leading to the path and turn right, facing upwards towards the deserted area. We start our uphill journey, which shouldn't take that long. But that still doesn't stop Noeleen from dragging her feet and complaining about it.

'Ohhhh, Mike, let's just go to the other path instead of up this hill.'

'Please, Noeleen, don't complain. We have to get out of here, no matter how much walking we do; we will eventually find a way out.'

'I'm sorry,' she says. 'I'm just tired.'

Fair enough; she's tired. But still, I don't complain every two minutes, and she's had more rest then I have.

As we keep moving, I keep noticing things I investigated when I first got here – the boulders, for example. I don't bother mentioning them to Noeleen; instead, we continue walking until, eventually, we get to the top.

'Wow, that was a bit steep for me,' she says.

'Come on; it wasn't that bad,' I reply, slapping her bum as she kneels down with both her hands on her knees to catch her breath.

She huffs and puffs for a while. I just gaze into the distance, the vast desert in front of me. Behind me, a beautiful world and the split of the two paths in the distance.

The deserted area has nothing special about it; it's full of dead trees and a lake that looks like it's filled with black tar. Nothing reflects off the surface. I decide to sit down on the soft turquoise grass, which will give

Noeleen a chance to rest. Sitting here is very comfortable, and the air is slightly chilled and fresh; it feels like my face is being sprayed with cool water, even though I'm not actually getting wet.

'Are you okay, sweetheart?'

'Thanks for asking. I'm still a little shaky from that attack earlier. I thought you were going to leave me here all alone. I wouldn't have been safe on my own. Thanks for being so protective also. You care so much about me.'

I grab her hand and hold it between my palms. I look into her eyes, smiling at her. 'Don't worry," I say. 'I'm not going anywhere just yet, you know. You will be stuck with me for quite a long time; unfortunate for you I think.'

'Don't be silly. I'm lucky to have met you. I wouldn't change this situation for anything else.'

'You are too cute, sweet Noeleen.'

She blushes and looks down. I must be embarrassing her again. She seems to still be quite shy around me, although she seems to be warming up at the same time. Sex with her was amazing, and for her to do it with me, she must have felt totally comfortable around me.

The grass here is so nice to touch, so soft. I keep stroking it hard with the palm of my hand. Each blade of grass stands tall, and it looks like it gets mowed every now and then. I'm curious about who else lives in this world.

'What would you say if I said let's go and check out that lake?' I ask. I expect her to complain.

'Do we have to? Well, you will anyway, so I might as well follow.'

Okay, she is getting used to me now. Brilliant. I don't need to convince her at all. I stand up, holding my hands out so she can hold them and I can help her up. I pull her up, and we both just stare into the distance past the lake, where there seems to be nothing but sand.

I make the first initiative to move forward and step onto the sand. She follows me, and we walk at a fast pace.

'Mike, look behind you.' She says with an excited tone. 'The ground is changing wherever we walk!'

I look behind me at the ground. *Wow!*

Our every footstep has turned into a grassy patch. As we stand together on the same spot, I notice the slow transformation from sand to grass. It's truly magical, and I cannot explain what's going on.

CHAPTER 20

From Desolation to Splendour

Each step we take changes into a small, shoe-shaped bit of grassland, my footsteps bigger than Noeleen's. I kneel down and place my palm on the sand, pressing as hard as I can.

As time passes, the sand becomes a grassy handprint. What a strange world. I thought I had seen everything, but this? This is truly something spectacular and out of the ordinary.

Lido runs around in circles, leaving grass footprints behind. By the time we get to the lake, we've left a nice trail of grass in our wake. The lake itself is calm, as there is no wind here. And it seems nothing would be able to live in it. The water is jet black, and I doubt it's water at all.

I place my hand in the water. My eyes open wide in amazement. 'Woahhhh. What is happening here?'

'I'm not sure, but wow.'

As soon as I touched the water, the lake ripples from my hand, and as the ripples get larger, the water is coming to life. Slowly, as the ripples move out, the water becomes crystal clear, so clear that, eventually, I can actually see the bottom. The lake bed is covered in crystals of all kinds;

they're scattered everywhere. And plants seem to be growing at a very rapid rate. Thickets of beautifully coloured species of plants are sprouting and growing in a matter of minutes.

From a desolate boring lake, this has become a beautiful lake filled with life.

Lido doesn't hang around but dives straight in, splashing me and Noeleen with the cool, clean fresh water. Following Lido, I jump into the water and swim around.

I splash Noeleen.

'Ahhhh. Mike, it's cold.'

'No it's not. Jump in!'

'No way am I doing that,' she says

'Suit yourself then. Have a seat on the sand. Don't worry. It will turn into grass in a few minutes,' I say.

This water is just perfect to swim in. I let my body go and leave myself to float. Lido swims under me, and I gaze at his beautiful colouration as he jumps over me. His tail whips up fresh water that splashes me in the face – a cooling refreshment for my dry skin and a bit of exercise for Lido.

I take this time to enjoy a swim. It's been a while since I've done a bit of a workout. I dive to the bottom and grab a handful of the beautiful crystals and swim to the shore, leaving them beside Noeleen.

'They're beautiful,' she shouts.

'This lake is full of those crystals. These few moments make me want to stay in this world and never return to my crappy life. Come on, join me.'

Once again, I splash water at Noeleen, soaking her from the front.

'Mike, I told you not to do that,' she yells.

'Oh, come on. It's just a bit of fun, sweetheart.'

What is her issue? I can understand that she wants to get out of here, but who wouldn't want to swim in such a beautiful clear lake? It's not like it's poisonous or anything like that.

Lido and I swim and dive together. Lido is much faster than me, I can't keep up. It doesn't make a difference. It's the most fun I've had since I've been here.

'Miiiiike, let's gooooooo.'

My god, she is moaning. It drives me insane. Still, I do like her way of thinking and style, and to be fair, she doesn't moan as much as my ex did. So she is good in most aspects; plus, no one is perfect. Everyone has his or her own little flaws. I am 200 percent sure she hates my way of wanting to explore pretty much everything, but that's something she'll have to get used to over time I guess. I can't change my personality and will never change for anyone.

With pure annoyance, I say, 'Ohhhh, Noelleeen, just let me enjoy this day.'

'Fine, I will just sit here then, right??'

I wish she would relax and stop raising her voice at me. What can I do? It's been my only opportunity to relax here.

All I have to say is that this swim is bliss, and the water has relaxed my body. Being in this lake is absolutely therapeutic.

I swim to the shoreline of the lake and rest myself on the rocks with my legs submerged in the water. 'It's a shame you wouldn't join me, Noeleen.'

'I'm sorry. I don't really like swimming that much. We should get going.'

'No problem. I understand that you're bored. Could you do me a favour and step on the area where there's sand so it turns into a grassy area? That way, I won't get sand all over me when I get back out.'

'Yes sure.'

She stands up and starts moving around, covering the area near the shoreline. Slowly, the beach turns into grass, which allows me to get out of the lake and sit comfortably for a while to dry off.

My suit is soaking wet, and water drips off me while I sit. Noeleen waits patiently, and Lido stays in the lake, swimming gracefully while I check the inside pocket to make sure the diamond I collected from the cave is still in there. Luckily, it didn't fall out while I was swimming. I'm sure Noeleen would have made us go back to the cave to get another one.

'Shall we head off?' she says.

'Can you please stop asking me to get going every two minutes? I'm sorry, but it's really getting on my nerves.'

'Why are you talking to me like that?'

'I'm being polite. Let me relax. Give me five minutes.'

'*Fine.*'

I roll up my trousers and take my time to enjoy the breeze grazing my face. I sit with my legs submerged in water. Noeleen is definitely not a happy bunny right now. She doesn't understand how nice this refreshing water feels. A few minutes go by, and I decide it's time to move on.

'Let's go, and I am sorry for the way I spoke to you earlier.'

She kisses me on the cheek. 'I'm sorry too.'

I get up, and we start moving. It doesn't take Lido long to realise that we're on the move again. He follows.

As we walk, water drips down me, wetting the sand and the old grass footprints we left behind. The grass still grows at every step we take. I decide to make my way towards the nearest dead tree, and I hug it. Magically, the tree comes to life. From the base of the bark, the tree, which looks similar to a palm tree, starts taking colour. The trunk is long and very tall. I gaze upwards at the leaves, which are huge, the size of a human; fold out from the middle, very similar to banana trees; and are orange at the tips and yellow at the base where they start growing. The bark is covered in little blue fruit the size of golf balls that give off a nice smell. The smell itself forces me to eat one.

'Mmm, Noeleen, come try one of these,' I shout.

'What are they?'

I chuck one at her. She catches it well.

'Nice catch, babe.'

'Do I have to peel it?' she asks.

'No, no. I just ate it how it is!'

She hesitates a little but then shuts her eyes as she bites into the tasty morsel. Juice from the fruit leaks out onto her hand and drips down. 'Mmmm, very nice. Bring some with you,' she says.

She comes over and cuts a few down, placing them in the backpack.

'We should make this place look nice before we head off!' she says.

'Yeah, okay. Let's split up and touch as much as possible. The trees can be hugged.'

She jogs away from me, going from one tree to another hugging them. I do the same. Also, I drag my feet so that I turn most of the sand into grass. Slowly, this place has life. Noeleen doesn't hang about, but she's already covered a huge area, and it seems some kinds of birds are already coming here. One kind with a very long beak and beautiful colours looks tropical. They hover at the bark and peck at the fruit attached to it, seemingly masters of flight.

As I stand looking at this amazing bird, Noeleen has actually made the place look amazing. I look back at the area, and she has made a difference. In fact, we have made this a place where creatures can flourish. How? I can't be sure, but that's the best thing about this situation. I don't have to question it, as I'll never get an answer.

'*Noeleen!*' I shout at the top of my voice.

'Yes?'

'Come here.'

I gesture for her, and she walks over.

'Let's get out of here. We've had enough fun now,' I say.

'Sounds like a plan.'

We start walking again. We get to the top of the path and gaze at what once was a deserted area, beautiful now with patches of grassland and plants, tall trees, and even some birds. I turn round and point at the second path, which will be our next destination.

'The view looks beautiful Mike. There seems to be a lot of wildlife there.'

'Don't be afraid, sweetheart. They're probably gentle creatures like Lido.'

She seems to be keeping a distance from me.

'Why the distance, Noeleen?'

'I don't want to get wet, thank you.'

I immediately start chasing her around with open arms.

'Ahhh! Stop it, Mike.'

I don't stop and keep chasing her down the hill.

She stops suddenly, forcing me to stop.

'Mike, don't even dare come close to me.'

'Why are you being so uptight?'

'I am not being uptight. I just don't want to get wet.'

I let her be, and we keep walking down the hill.

'I'm sorry for being so annoying sometimes,' I say.

'It's okay. You don't have to worry. I like it. But still, I don't want to get wet.'

'I understand, sweetheart.'

She is quite hard-headed and seems to like to get her way, but I don't mind. I like everything about her. The comfortable rock at the bottom of the path is in our view, and it doesn't take long for us to get there. The path on the right is very similar to the path on the left. Both seem man-made, and both have hedges on each side – like they were meant to be like that. Here, too, we find cut hedge leaves scattered on the ground, as if someone trimmed the hedges. Why and who is still a mystery at this point, but I'm sure we'll find out.

'Do you think this is the way out?' she asks.

'Yes, I'm really positive about this.'

'Good.'

We continue our journey downhill towards the end of the path. My suit is still wet, but it's slowly drying out. Noeleen rushes past me as we pass hundreds of insects swarming some of the bushes.

The end of the path is visible, and beyond that, we can't see much, as the hedges on either side of the path tower over us, blinding our vision. The path itself is exactly the same as the other one we've been on and is even made of the same type of stone. It looks quite symmetrical.

'Do you have any childhood dreams, Mike?' she asks.

'Not really,' I tell her. 'I didn't have such a great childhood. But at one point, I wanted to study business and marketing.'

'What happened?' she asks.

'It's a long story, and I don't want to talk about my past at the moment.' It's too emotional, and this is not the place to be talking about my past. Maybe if I feel comfortable later, I will give her my whole story. I definitely don't feel like it at the moment. Too much has happened, and I'd need to sit down to tell that story.

'No problem, Mike.'

At least she doesn't press me to elaborate on this emotional subject and just lets me be. She looks a tad disappointed when I don't say anything to her. Deep down, she really wants to know what happened. But I can't start talking about it now.

We get to the end of the path.

'Stop here for a few minutes,' I say.

'Okay.'

I need to evaluate our position and what we will be facing soon. I don't want any danger coming our way.'

I gaze to my right. A beautiful open field lies ahead. I see what look like flowers everywhere and huge creatures congregating in herds. To the left of the field, I see rock, a valley, and a path going uphill, though the path is grass and doesn't seem to be cut. Adjacent to this grass are rows of trees and just pure tranquil beauty. The meadow seems well taken care of.

The sky to my right is full of bird-like creatures, diving and flying back up again. The sun seems to be high up in the sky, and I pick out three of the moons. All seem to be at a distance. They look very similar to our moon, although the one that's farthest away looks green and probably has an atmosphere. These are the same moons I've seen before. The moon that looks like earth could be very similar to this place – teeming with life and gorgeous views.

'Parts of this world remind me of the Amazon,' I say.

'You've been to the Amazon?'

'Yeah, my ex and I took a trip there once.'

The diversity of species is plentiful there. It makes me appreciate what our earth has to offer.

'Nice. I'd like to go to the Maldives one day – gorgeous islands. And the sun is scorching there,' she explains.

'Yeah, I wouldn't mind. Shall we keep moving?'

'Yes.'

CHAPTER 21

A Deep Cavern

We all plod along down the path. As we move to the left towards what seems to be a valley, we chat about different places we would like to travel to. We seem to have the same tastes, and she seems quite the travelling kind of person.

'Where abouts have you been?' I ask.

'I've been to China and the USA. Haven't been to many places, as I had to save for both holidays. I went with a group of friends. China was beautiful, and the USA was just for shopping.'

'Ahhh nice, would love to go to China one day.'

'Yeah, you would love the Great Wall, although a lot of walking is involved.'

'No different than being here then, eh.'

All this relaxed talking seems to have gotten me into a pickle, as I realise too late that I've fallen into what seems to be some kind of trap. I push Noeleen away as my foot plunges through the ground.

'Miiiiike!'

'Ahhhhhhhhh!'

I'm going down a slide of sorts and land in a pool of water underground. Noeleen peeks through the hole. 'Mike, can you hear me?' she shouts. Her voice echoes around.

'Yes, I can hear you,' I tell her. 'I'm in a pool of water, and I'm safe. Don't worry about me. You need to get to the rocky area and go into what seemed like a valley. Can you do that for me?'

'Yes, Mike, but I'm terrified,' she says.

'Don't worry. Lido is with you, I'm going to try and find a way out, and I'll come to that valley. Wait there, okay. You should be safe. I'll do whatever I can to find you.'

'Okay, Mike. Please take care of yourself. See you soon.'

'See you soon, sweetheart.'

I swim towards a rocky area in front of me. The water is very cold down here, and I won't be able to take it for much longer. I get to the rocky shore of the pool and pull the torch out of my backpack, hoping it still works. I click it on, and luckily, it shines. The torch lights up the view in front of me. What look like stalactites and stalagmites protrude from the ground and the ceiling. In front of me are a few rock formations, which I climb slowly, ensuring I don't hurt myself.

Nothing inhabits this cave, and the smell is quite potent. It feels like some kind of acid brews down here, as my eyes water slightly.

I climb up the rock, grabbing onto any crack in the bedrock that supports my weight. Eventually, I make it up there. The entire cave is blocked off, but there seems to be a small passageway through to the next part. I shout through the hole, and hear my voice echo from the other side. I have to squeeze through a little gap, which is big enough. But given that I'm quite claustrophobic, I hesitate. Taking deep breaths in to stop myself from panicking, I hold the torch in my mouth and push myself through the gap with my legs, moving my arms slowly to help myself out of the tight gap. Eventually I make it through. This part of the underground cavern is very dangerous, with lots of obstacles in my way.

The climb down is much easier than the climb up on the other side. Still, as I make my way down, I keep losing my footing, as rock crumbles beneath my feet.

It's a relief when my foot touches the hard ground and I can actually keep moving forward. I move around gigantic stalagmites. Some of the stalagmites and stalactites join to make a column. I press my hand on one, and it feels very sticky – and not a nice kind of sticky. 'Yuck!'

I wipe my hand onto my trousers, and the sticky substance comes off quite easily, but until I find another pool of water, I won't be able to cleanse my hands fully. I sit down to listen to my surroundings, and in the distance, I can hear a waterfall. I aim to get there and clean my viscous hands, and hopefully, there'll be a way out of here. Nothing seems interesting down here, and someone definitely made that trap; the hole was a perfect circle covered with turf.

I keep thinking about Noeleen, and I hope she's safe and sound. I'm not too worried, as Lido is with her. But the fact that I may not see her again makes me sick to my stomach. As much as she moans a lot, I miss having her being by my side. She keeps me going and keeps me smiling. I miss Lido too.

I'm sure there is a way out. The waterfall has to come from above. I just hope I can climb against the water coming down, and I hope the climb isn't too steep.

I start moving again, trying to avoid the stalagmites, stalactites, and columns; my feet seem to stick to the ground slightly with every step I take, which slows me down dramatically. The surface is so sticky it's a struggle to walk. The smell, which is getting unbearable, must be coming from this stuff. I'm forced to tear a piece of my shirt off and use that to cover my face. It's wet and very cold, and my body shivers as I walk.

I notice a small pool no bigger than a bucket of water. I go towards it and kneel down to investigate. I use a couple of fingers to check the consistency.

Wow, this stuff is very sticky. I wonder what it is.

I rub my fingers together; this stuff seems to be no different from glue. I point the torch at the pool, and the liquid is dark green. It's very slimy, and nothing could live in it. In fact, it irritates my finger slightly.

Is this some kind of acid?

I ask myself questions, hoping someone will answer. There's definitely nothing but me down here. Now and again, an odd rock falls from the ceiling, making a loud ticking sound that echoes throughout this underground hellhole.

As much as I try to avoid touching anything, it seems to be inevitable, and my hands are feeling rather mucky and sticky. My suit trousers seem heavier as more and more material adds to them. The sticky stuff dries quickly, considering how humid it is down here, and it's becoming quite a task to walk in them. Where they are torn, the trousers are stuck to my legs, as some of the gluey liquid has entered through the tear.

I try to pull the trousers, so they won't be stuck to my leg anymore. 'Ouch. Wow this feels like I'm waxing my legs. Noeleen will have to help me out of them.'

If I ever find her that is. God knows what she's doing right now. Probably cowering in a corner, scared on her own. Lido is probably jumping around being Lido.

I flash my torch in front of me. The waterfall sounds are getting nearer and nearer. It won't be that far now. I just have to get over these last obstacles in the way, and I'll finally be able to wash all this glue off of me. I clutch onto the rock, climb onto it, and jump onto the next one, my right foot nearly slipping off the edge.

'Phew, that was close.'

A shot of adrenaline is released into my bloodstream, and my heart rate increases rapidly. I look down in between the two rocks; all I see is pointed stalagmites. If I'd fallen in there, it would have been certain death for me, and Noeleen wouldn't even know about it.

I stand tall on this huge boulder and stare into the distance, the torch in my right hand pointing at the waterfall. A large pool where the waterfall ends fills quite a large area. I climb down onto the rock substrate below me and feel the water.

Wow, this is surprisingly warmish.

I walk down into the pool and wash myself from top to bottom. I scrub my legs with my fingertips, hoping the glue will come off and save me the pain of waxing my legs later. It doesn't take long but eventually comes off, and I feel all nice and clean again.

I swim towards where the water cascades from above to look for a way up, grateful to see light pouring down from the hole. The waterfall itself isn't that powerful, and behind it, some vines lead out of this place. I tug on the vines to make sure they're secure, and they barely budge. I start to climb, holding my breath as water falls onto my face. Now and again, I lean back as far as I can to take in some air. Slowly but surely, I'll be back out of this place. I place one foot in between two vines for stability and use my other foot to push myself up so I can grab onto the next set of vines.

It doesn't take me long to climb up, and I grab onto the ground, clutching onto the grass and pull myself up.

At last, I got out of there.

In front of me, a few metres away, Noeleen sits facing the opening of the valley she came through, presumably waiting for my return.

She just sobs to herself. 'Michael where are you? I have been waiting here for a while now, and I need you beside me.'

Lido runs towards me, wagging his tail.

'Noeleeeen.'

'Miiiiike.'

She gets up and runs towards me and hugs me.

'I'm all wet, you know.'

'I don't care. I'm so happy that you're safe. What was down there?'

'Nothing special,' I say.

'I'm so glad you're back. I thought something terrible happened.'

She cries, presumably with happiness that I'm back, still holding onto me as if I will run away from her. I feel badly that she's crying, but she has nothing to cry about, so I say nothing but comfort her. This shows she actually cares about me, and Lido seems to have missed me too, as he climbs onto my leg nudging at me to stroke him.

'Lido, I've missed you, buddy.'

Rrrrrrrrrrrrrrrrrrrrrrrrrrrrrrrrrrrraaaaaaaaaaaaaaaaaaaarrrrrrrrrrrrrrrrrrrrrr.

'He seems way too excited,' I say.

'We have missed you, eh,' she says through her sobs.

'Did you encounter any trouble while you were making your way here?'

'Not really, although I got scared because of some kind of crab look alike creature. Lido seemed to like eating those,' she adds.

'I'll have to investigate later, eh.'

I am so glad to be back in her company again. It seemed like I was down there forever and that I would never get out. But, some things aren't what they seem, and you should never give up on what you need to do. I certainly haven't, and here I am with my prize, Noeleen. I would never give up on her, even if it meant certain death. Spending time with this girl has really made me soft. It feels like it's my first love, but it also feels like we've been in love forever.

'Noeleen, you don't have to hold me so tight. I'm not going anywhere,' I whisper.

'But' She nuzzles against my chest. 'You said that once before, and this world split us apart. I don't want that to happen again. I didn't feel safe on my own.'

'Don't worry. Nothing in this world or our world will tear us apart. As long as our feelings stay strong, nothing will be able to break that,' I say.

'Ohhh, I know what you mean.'

She kisses me on the neck, still not letting go of me. Everything that's happened to her here – from nearly being attacked to me disappearing – has definitely shaken her up. Now she has me in her arms, and I won't leave her again. I am sure nothing will change the way I feel about her.

I pull her away from me and place my hand on her face. 'Don't worry, Noeleen. I'm right in front of you. Don't be scared. I'm right here.'

I decide to place my backpack on the ground, as it needs to dry out. And as I am still soaked and have nothing to dry my face and hair with, I decide to stay in this valley for a while. The place seems safe, and I doubt anything would attack us in here. Lido stands guard anyway.

'Oh, poor Lido; we depend on him so much,' she says out of the blue.

'Well, to be fair, he has been there for both of us. And if it wasn't for him, we'd be goners, eh.'

'Yes. Are you still cold, Mike? I noticed you where shivering earlier!'

Ah, again, she's showing she cares for me. I blush and reply, 'I'm okay, thanks to your snuggly hug.'

The front of her dress is all wet, and she doesn't seem to be bothered. I think she's just glad I turned up.

'You should dry up soon, sweetheart,' I say.

'It's okay. It's quite refreshing.'

Wow, she has changed her tone quite a bit, I think, recalling how earlier she didn't want to get wet at all. She's just one of a kind. Despite the few little things I don't like, there are way more things I love about her.

We just stand there talking, without a care in the world. Something just doesn't feel right here though. It's like I can feel the ground moving slightly.

CHAPTER 22

The Light

'Noeleen, did you feel that?'

'No. What happened?'

'Surely you felt that?' How could she not feel that tremor? It wasn't huge, but I definitely am not crazy, and I felt it. Why are these things happening to me? Am I really going crazy? I seem to be, according to what's happening.

'Are you okay?' she says as she holds on to both my shoulders.

'I'm okay, just felt a bit of a tremor; quite strange, considering you didn't feel anything.'

I feel very drowsy, as if I'm going to pass out again. I shut my eyes for a few seconds, trying to clear my mind of all thoughts, and open them again.

'Noeleeeen!'

'Michael, I'm right in front of you.'

'No you're not; you have disappeared,' I say in a voice full of fright.

'You're right in front of me. Are you okay? You're starting to scare me a little.'

'Don't be afraid. I can't see you anymore. I'm not near you at all.'

'What do you mean? Your body is right here!' She screams as she panics.

What she keeps saying seems to suggest that I have gone completely nuts and need psychiatric assistance. What is happening to me? I'm in a room alone; it's all white with writing on the walls. Everywhere I look, I see the same paragraph, the same words. It's not in English and appears to be Latin. The room is lit in a bright white light, and the black writing seems to be magically imprinted on the wall.

'Noeleen, are you still near me?'

I think she's freaking out, as the tone of her voice has just changed. 'Yes, I am, but you're starting to freak me out. You're looking at me.'

'You have to listen to me okay. My body is there, but I'm not there. I'm in a room that's lit very brightly, and there seems to be writing all over the wall. I think it's in Latin.'

'But …'

She doesn't believe me. I'm not making this up. I sit down on the hard ground. Looking around, I see that all four walls are exactly symmetrical, and the floor is the same too. It seems as if I'm in a square room. 'But nothing,' I say. 'You have to believe me. Please don't leave my side until I come back. Is my body moving at all?'

'No, it just stands there.'

'Can you slap me please?'

'Slap you?' she says

'*Yes* –as hard as you can in the face, okay,' I yell.

'Ok, ready? Here it goes'

Ouch. That actually hurt, and I definitely heard the sound of the slap. All I keep asking myself throughout this weird adventure is what the hell? Someone has sent me here to piss me off. I start following the letters on the ground with my index finger, trying to make out the words.

'Desine in conspectum praeterita et futura vivere felix et adimpleretur'

'What are you talking about, Mike?'

'These are the words written all over the walls of this room. Sounds like Latin. Are you familiar with any of the words I just said?'

'Say them again please, read the words slowly so I can jot them down on the notepad. Give me a second to get what I need.' She rustles through the bag to find a pen.

'Go for it Mike, I'm ready.'

'Okay. Here it goes. Desine in conspectum praeterita et futura vivere felix et adimpleretur.' I can barely say the words, so I hope she understood.

She stays silent for a while. 'Uh, I'm not too sure, but I can make out some of the words,' she finally says.

'Really?'

'Yes, Latin is the root of many different languages, and I know some languages.'

'Okay, Noeleen, tell me what you think.'

'From what you said, I can make out, stop your something? And in your future life, something happy and fulfilling. I don't know. Let me think for a while. Hmmmmm.'

I give her time to think about it, as I have no idea what the inscription says. In the meantime, I take my time to look around and get used to this room. I feel quite intrigued to know what the inscription says. At the same time, I'm freaked out. But at least I'm used to this freaky world. *Nothing new, to be honest*, I realise. *Seen worse here.* Like breathing under the ocean – that was fun up until I got myself paralyzed.

I stand upright and move towards the nearest wall, placing my palm against it. The wall feels slightly warm from the heat of the light and feels like glass. The inscription seems to be written behind the glass. By this, I can actually tell how thick the glass is – around the thickness of a DVD case – and no way can I break it bare fisted. A hammer would smash the wall, but on this occasion, my backpack isn't on me, so I have no tools. I reach into my pockets. Nothing, the keys aren't there, and all I can feel is dust and lint.

I remember that I have pockets on the inside of the jacket. I fold one side of the suit jacket over and reach into the pocket. What's that? Feels like I have something in there – some kind of stone. I pull it out. It's the diamond I got for Noeleen earlier. Being playful and curious, I should test it to see if it is a diamond. Kneeling down, I place the pointed part of the diamond against the glass, drag it, and press down, making a screeching sound. It is actually scratching the glass.

'Noeleen, the diamond is actually a real diamond.'

'Oh, Mike, you just lost me. I nearly had the whole translation, and now I forgot what I was translating. Please stay quiet, and don't make so much noise, I need to study what I have written.' she says.

Wow she's being slightly stern; at least she's interested in something other than getting out of here. Maybe she has gotten used to the fact that there's no way out, and maybe this is a good challenge for her. Twiddling my thumbs I have no idea what to do next. I tend to get very bored easily. 'What to do, what to do!'

I can hear her voice again, and she doesn't seem happy. 'Will you keep your mouth shut for a minute?'

Did she just shout at me?

'Let me think in peace,' she says.

Oh very strict, isn't she? At least I found something she's interested in. She didn't have to shout though. I don't think she would be quiet if she was stuck in here. I bet she'd be screaming for help. *Michael, get me out of here!* It's not normal to be stuck in a room with a stupid inscription everywhere.

I take some time to relax and contemplate what the hell is going on. I start thinking about her. She's too good to be true; it isn't normal for me to meet someone who respects me for who I am or accepts the way I am. Even after seeing my house, she still treats me the same.

'Psssst, Mike, still there?'

'Yes, Noeleen? Did you come up with something?'

'Not yet, just wanted to say something,' she says.

'What's up?'

'Nothing,' she whispers.

My curiosity kicks in again. 'Oh, don't do that; you know how curious I get. What did you want to say?'

'Ermmmm.'

'Come on spit it out, sweet.'

'Mike?'

'Yes?' I say, eager to know what she has to say.

'I miss you.'

Oh my god; she misses me. Not sure what to say, I feel a sudden rush of blood to my face, blushing and feeling a sense of warmth. A giant smile crosses my face, and I feel chemicals rushing through my body. My heart is pounding harder, and I feel like a little boy again with my first love. 'I miss you too, you know,' I say in a gentle voice.

'Sorry, that kind of came out; didn't want to make you feel uncomfortable,' she explains.

'No, no. That really made me smile, you know.'

'Aw. Mike, you are so sweet.'

I guess everyone finds someone in the end – someone who loves them no matter what, someone who accepts everything about them. Is that not what love is?

'How long till you finish translating the inscription?' I ask her.

'Well, so far, I think it says, 'Stop dwelling on your past and live happy and fulfilling.'

The inscription starts to fade away. A few seconds pass and it reappears again. 'Noeleen the inscription was fading when you were saying it. Then it came back. I think if we figure it out, I'll be out of here.'

'Okay, let me work on it a little longer. I'm still using the notepad; hope you don't mind,' she says.

'No, no, carry on. I'll just wait here.' I place the diamond back in the inside of my jacket pocket.

I sit down with my back against the glass wall. It isn't that comfortable, and the light is giving me a slight headache. I close my eyes and relax for a while, giving her all the time she needs to crack the code. Maybe sometime today, we can continue our journey out of this place.

All these messages and codes – are they trying to tell me something about my life? I think so. That makes a bit of sense if I think about it. This world is opposite of mine. Even those Post-it notes on the fridge saying,

'Get out' could fit; maybe they were telling me to get out of my miserable life and out of that grotty house.

'Stop dwelling on your past and live a happy and fulfilled future,' she shouts out of the blue.

CHAPTER 23

Puzzle

The writing on the wall goes faint as she talks and then disappears. I'm still in here.

What is going on? New writing has replaced the other phrase. What kind of joke is this? Looks like I'm in a puzzle, which is testing my patience.

'Mike … You're not back here, are you?'

Annoyance and anger bubble up deep within me. 'Sorry, but now new writing has come up.'

She laughs as if I said something hilarious. 'Oh wicked. I'm loving this game. Tell me what it says.'

It's not really that funny to be truthful; there is nothing for me to do in here except sit. And think about things I don't wish to think about.

'*Omnis moritur, sed non omnis vivit.*'

'I know this,' she claims.

'What is it?'

'No. Sorry. Forget it; it's not what I thought. I don't have any idea to be honest. I need some time.'

She got my hopes up there, for nothing. But I do not know any languages, let alone latin, so cannot be too critical on her. I stay silent, mute for a while, restraining myself from screaming out loud. I don't want to interrupt her precious thoughts. I hold onto hope she'll translate this inscription – meaningful words that might change our lives. Who knows? For once, I feel dumb, stupid more like; I have no idea how to go about translating these paragraphs. I'm helpless and have no interest in this place. I'm just sitting here staring at my trousers, all torn at the knees and covered in grass stains. My shirt is scuffed, torn at the bottom, and no longer tucked in

Somehow I feel like a tramp. But surprisingly, I do not stink at all. I haven't had a shower since I've been here, except for the few occasions when I went swimming, but I still smell good. Strange world. This could mean that bacteria don't grow here, and technically speaking, if I had a loaf of bread, it wouldn't go mouldy. Now this intrigues me. I'd like to try my theory out. But guess what? I have no bread and no kind of food. The food I had in my briefcase disappeared along with the case.

'Any luck on this new puzzle, Noeleen?'

Nothing. I wonder if she's still there.

'Noeleeenn?' I shout out loud.

'Mike, you don't have to shout. I'm still here trying to figure out the inscription.'

'Well, why didn't you say anything then? I can't see you, and I worry easily,' I explain.

'Sorry. I was just deep in concentration. I need some time. Why don't you have a nap?'

'*Really*!? You think I can nap here? I think not, sweetheart. But I'm a patient guy; I'll wait. Continue what you were doing. I won't interrupt again.'

'Aw, thank you. You are such a babe.' She giggles and then goes silent again, presumably trying to work out the inscription. Nothing else she could be doing. I haven't heard from Lido; he must be asleep. It isn't usual for him to take such long naps. He usually runs around like a child.

I look around me, amazed at the science of this place. Where did it all come from? Who built this? I have so many questions I want answered, and I'm afraid no one will be here to answer them for me. The best I can do is explore and speculate.

I take a deep breath in – such clean air for a contained room. It feels fresh in here and slightly on the cold side. I wrap my suit jacket around me and button it up, tuck my shirt in, and tighten my belt. I place my hands on my biceps and rub hard to warm up. Every time I exhale, I see the condensation from my breath.

'I'm cold,' I say, shivering.

'Aw, Mike. If only I was there; I'd warm you up. Why not think of that night we had back at your place? That should warm you up.'

I laugh. 'Sounds like a plan. Mmmm, your naked body against mine.'

'Imagine me kissing your neck and imagine my tongue rubbing all over your sexy chest,' she says.

Mmm, so kinky. That will definitely warm me up. I imagine her sliding her tongue down my chest and pull back so she is looking at me, grinding her teeth together – that naughty look that arouses me so much.

'You've gone silent.' Her sexy voice echoes all over the room.

'Just thinking, beautiful,' I reply.

'No fair. You should get back here and show me your thoughts.'

The thoughts take me back to the flat where I was on top of her, pleasuring her. She moaned as I was deep inside her. I remember the way I made her want me more and more, teased her until she couldn't take it much longer. She is so sexy and makes me feel so hot.

Wow, I'm actually feeling warm again. I feel like playing with myself, but there is no way I'm getting it out here. I don't want to degrade myself. Someone might be watching through the glass, laughing at me as I'm stuck in here.

'How's the inscription translation coming along?'

'You know what? At first I didn't know what this was all about, but I think I'll soon be able to translate it. How are your thoughts coming along?'

I laugh out loud. 'Ermmmmmm, you just made me blush,' I reply.

'You don't need to be shy, boo.'

Boo? That's new. She is so adorably incredible. Her personality just gleams through me. I want her more and more by the second.

'Rarrrrrrrrrrrrrrrrrrrrrrrrrrrr.'

'Lido is awake?'

'Yes, and he seems rather interested in the backpack for some reason. He keeps scratching at it and looking at me,' she explains.

'Strange. Ignore it for now. Keep trying to translate so I can be near you again.'

Lido seems to be going mental; maybe he has noticed that I'm not actually there? Or who knows what he's thinking? He's only an animal at the end of the day. Why is he scratching at the backpack? If only Lido knew how to speak Latin ...

I start whistling, hoping Lido will respond.

'Hey, boy. Lidooooooooo. How did he react to me calling him?'

'Not much really. He looked at your body and continued scratching at the backpack. Is he hungry, Mike?'

'Not sure, sweet. Will have to find him some food when I come back, eh. Mind you, he is actually good at catching his own meals. He caught this huge fish creature before and was nudging it towards me. I tried it, and it tasted alright. I'm sure you noticed that carcass near the lake. That was Lido's catch.'

'Wow, a handy creature, isn't he?'

She sounds too cute when she talks. At least she's not stressing out too much. She's definitely come in handy on this occasion. I hope she cracks the code soon. I'm sick of being in here. So boring and nothing to see. Now I am lying on the floor with one of my arms behind my head, staring at the ceiling. I'm looking for some clue as to what's going on. Nothing seems abnormal, other than the fact I'm in here. There must be some kind of mechanism that changed the words in the room. I keep wondering what's behind the glass. Some powerful light bulbs, that's for sure, to emit so much light.

I start feeling slightly uncomfortable lying on the hard ground, so I change position and lie on my side, my elbow resting on the glass and the palm of my hand cupping my head for support. I yawn but not because I'm tired. Must be a lack of oxygen in the room. It isn't ventilated after all, so no fresh air can come in and replace the carbon dioxide I breathe out.

Lido seems to be going crazy out there; I wonder what he wants. I hope Noeleen isn't in danger, but I'm not too worried; that creature can sure pack a strong punch. He's an aggressive little thing, and yet he's cute and shows such affection towards me and Noeleen. His colouration is just amazing, and the patterns on his body are out of this world – nothing like what exists back home.

'Uh, Noeleen ...'

'Sorry, I've become distracted by Lido. I need more time. I'm trying to think of this phrase, as I've heard someone say it once before,' she explains.

'Interesting, where did you hear it?'

'It was at my university. Law students learn some Latin. But this one particular girl, Natasha, was the brightest most knowledgeable person I knew at that time. She was brilliant – straight A's and always at the top of her classes. She had no social life and lived very comfortably at home, so she didn't have the stress of managing on her own. But I couldn't go without going out at least once a month, to be honest. I need to remember what she said about this Latin phrase; she definitely said it once. We were in the courtyard, and I was having a general conversation with her. This guy walked past her and said something to her. She replied with this Latin phrase. He didn't know what it meant, but she refused to tell him, and in the end, he walked off. But after he was gone, she told me what it meant, and I can't remember that part of the conversation,' she says.

She seems confused and dazzled. I'm surprised at how interested she is in languages. She doesn't talk about her life much; in fact she's been rather silent in that area. I hardly know her.

'Mike, I got it!'

'Go on then – *tell me*!' I stand up all excited, waiting to hear the translation – and get out of here at last.

'One sec; I think I got it wrong. Sorry, I'm not sure.' she says.

Not good; my hopes went up for nothing. Now I am all back to square one – waiting. I pace around the room for a while awaiting her translation. I brush my hand against the glass wall as I walk and huff and puff for a while. Knowing this won't do any good, I quickly calm back down, taking long breaths in.

She mutters to herself. 'Is it, every man dies, but not every man truly lives?'

'Noeleen, the written inscription was fading when you started saying it. Can you say it louder please?'

'Yes of course. See you soon. Every man dies, but not every man truly lives.'

As she finishes, the writing on the wall disappears, and the light brightens about hundred times brighter. The light swallows me whole. I cover my eyes with my arm. What is happening and what do the inscriptions mean to me?

'Psst, Mike, why are you covering your eyes?' she asks.

'Ohhh, yes, I'm back! As soon as you said the inscription out loud, the phrase and writing disappeared completely, and the light brightened.'

CHAPTER 24

My Past

Now I need to figure out what the inscriptions meant. *Stop dwelling on your past and live a happy fulfilled future. Every man dies, but not every man truly lives.*

My mind goes blank for a while.

Noeleen pokes me on the chest. 'Mike, come back to earth.'

'Oh sorry, I blanked out for a second there, didn't I?'

'Yes you did,' she answers.

'Sorry. Just thinking about the inscriptions and what they mean.'

'Definitely something to do with your life, as you ended up stuck in there,' she says.

'Hmmm so what do they mean? Yes, fine, my past wasn't so great. Both my parents died in a car accident, and I hardly have any family. I remember it as if it was yesterday. I was only seven years old. I was sitting in the back seat of a Vauxhall Astra. The paint on the side of the car was all scratched, as Mum scraped the side of the car while parking. I remember innocently playing with a toy dinosaur in the back; my parents were in the front. Dad was driving, and they were having a small argument about money. Next to me, I had a bottle of drink and my little rucksack that I used to love. It all happened so quickly.'

I look down, as the feeling that I'm going to cry heightens, clenching both my fists and shaking my head slowly. Noeleen tilts my head up with her finger tips, so I'm looking at her. I smile, definitely a fake smile, and I think she can tell. She grabs my wrists, pulls me close to her, hugs me, holding me close and rubbing my back gently.

'It's okay. You don't have to continue with the story. I see it's making you very sad. This is the first time I've seen you like this, and it's not a nice feeling, although I can understand what you went through. Maybe those inscriptions are trying to tell you something.'

She does make me feel better, and I feel I can open up fully to her. It isn't normal for me to cry, but she makes me feel like I can with her and that she will not judge me no matter what. She is a mature woman, who is understanding and caring. I push her away from me and smile at her.

'Thank you,' I say.

She smiles back, giving me a warm feeling deep inside. 'No problem.'

'Would you like to hear the rest of the story?'

'Yes, please go on. I am happy to stand here. I don't feel like sitting, but if you don't want to stand, then please sit down. I don't mind,' she answers.

'No, no, I'll stand too. Look at Lido. Why is he scratching at the bag?'

She grabs my hand and holds it between her palms. 'Forget about Lido for now. I would like you to pour it out; it will make you feel much better.'

'Okay, here goes. So there's me, sitting down playing with my rubber dinosaur toy; it was actually a triceratops, and it was all purple, and I had chewed off one of its horns. Mother and Father wanted to buy me a new one, but I didn't want one, as it was my favourite toy. I even slept with it near me.'

'I had a favourite toy too,' she mutters.

'What was it?' I ask.

'No continue with your story. I'm sorry for interrupting.'

'Please tell me. You aren't interrupting. In fact, every time you talk, your voice just sinks into my skin and makes me feel good about myself.'

'Mike, you are too good to me. It was only a My Little Pony toy.'

'Oh, yes, I know what you mean. They came in different colours, right?'

'Yes they did. You used to collect them, didn't you?' she says and laughs.

'Ahhh, don't make me bite you,' I say.

'Please continue with the story.'

'Okay, no problem. So, yeah, dinosaur in my hand, rucksack next to me, and like I said before, it happened so fast. Dad wasn't driving fast at all. In fact he never drove fast; he was always under the speed limit. I can't exactly remember what speed he was going, but I can tell you, it was slow. It used to take us ages to get to our destinations. My friends always teased me, especially on camping trips, where they would arrive way before us, and by the time we'd get there, their tents were up already. But he always made sure we were safe, and I can understand now why he always drove slowly. Mum, on the other hand, she wasn't such a good driver. Dad used to tell her off all the time because she wouldn't indicate properly and would cut corners all the time.'

'I don't understand why people speed to be honest,' she inserts.

'Anyway, I don't want to go out of point. Basically a car was coming the opposite way, and that driver was definitely speeding. He clipped his car against the corner of my parent's car, and our car just spun around a couple of times. I was knocked unconscious and don't know what happened after. But I woke up in a hospital all dazed and with a head wound all stitched up. My arm was broken, and my chest and abdominal region were bruised from the seat belt. I woke up with a drip in my arm and an oxygen mask. I had no idea of where I was. Nor did I know my parents were not there at all; in fact, they were dead. Neither the doctor nor the nurses told me what had happened until I gained full consciousness.'

'Wow, you went through a lot didn't you, Mike. I bet you were hurt, eh.'

At this point, I feel a tear trickling down my left cheek. Noeleen uses her thumb to wipe it off.

'Thanks for listening. Want to hear more?'

'Yes, please. I feel bad though.'

'It's okay. Things happen in life, and sometimes there's nothing we can do to help the situation,' I say, talking calmly and, now and again, sniffing as I cry.

'You're right.'

'I sobbed when they told me my parents had gone to heaven. I knew I'd never see them again. I was young, but I wasn't stupid at that age. I knew they had died. One of the nurses gave me my dinosaur back, and I remember hugging it so hard and so close to my chest. That day, I was changed. I went from being a happy boy to a miserable child. I never was told exactly what happened – how my parents died. I didn't need to know. I was too young to understand at that age. The doctors kept me in hospital for around two weeks to make sure I had recovered completely. My arm was in a cast and bandaged up. Nurses used to come and see me, as I had no visitors – no one to claim me at all. I was completely alone at that stage of my life. I had to grow up quickly. When I left, I was placed in an orphanage. I had to share a small bedroom with another child who was slightly older than me, around two years older, Timothy. His parents abandoned him at birth, and he had been living at the orphanage for nine years.'

'Did you get along with Timothy?'

'Well, yes and no. He didn't like that I was always sad and crying. And yes because we used to play together now and again. He was used to not having his parents around, so his life was a little bit easier in my opinion.'

'What was your room like?' she asks.

'It was okay, a bit small. The walls where painted light blue, and we had a very small TV. The bunk bed made a lot of noise at night, as it wasn't that sturdy, but I made do and got used to it. The carpet was horrid. I hated the colour. It was maroon with yellow dots and a silly pattern, but there was nothing we could do about the décor. The furniture was pine and very simple. Clothes we wore were from donations people gave to the orphanage, and the food they fed us was okay. But we were never allowed any sweets. Christmas was quite dull, but that was the time we got a chocolate bar. I remember making this one chocolate bar last a week, eating only a small bit every day.'

'Doesn't sound like a good orphanage,' she says.

'Well, it was an orphanage after all. They weren't obliged to feed us sweets and give us expensive clothes and gifts.'

God I hated those days. What a dump I lived in. What a dump I live in now. *Forget about all that, Mike.* I think about how maybe this world is trying to open my eyes a little so I can move on.

'Did you ever live with a family?' she asks.

'Yes actually. It didn't go so well.'

'Why not?'

'Well, I was eleven years old, and I remember how excited I was. The nuns at the orphanage told me that I was going to live with a nice family in the outskirts of the city. It didn't take long to pack my things. The family was going to pick me up that Friday, and by Thursday, I was ready to go. I thought, *Brilliant, I can't wait to meet my new potential brothers and sisters.*

Anyway, Friday morning came. I woke up extra early and did my morning routine. I ate some porridge and dragged out my packed things, which were packed in a black rubbish bag, by the way.'

'By the way—'

'Yes, sweetheart?'

'What happened to all your belongings that you had when your parents where alive?' she asks.

'Oh, yes, I missed that part. The house got repossessed, and all its contents were taken, as my parents owed a lot of money to debtors. They took everything, including my toys and clothes,' I explain.

'Oh, I understand. So what happened with the family then? You got picked up that Friday.'

'Yes, I did. So they picked me up and helped me with my bag. I still had the dinosaur, but it was packed in my rucksack. The family introduced themselves, and everyone seemed really nice. The mother was called Kath and, and the father was Anthony. They also had two children, Benjamin and Sarah. They were much older than me, but they all seemed like a nice family.'

'So what went wrong?' she asks.

'Well, they took me to their house, a beautiful house – four bedrooms and a huge kitchen. They even had a library, all in a contemporary décor, and my bedroom was big. I even had an en suite. But I wasn't used to all that luxury and was still a miserable child. As much as I was excited to be with a new family, I still didn't feel like I was at home, and I missed my parents so very much.'

'That's quite understandable. Did they not accept that?'

'No. After a while, they got sick of my bad moods and sent me back to the orphanage,' I explain.

'How rude. You would think they would understand what you went through.'

They just didn't understand at all. I could have had a really good life with them, but I still needed time to adjust to my bad situation. At the end of the day, it isn't easy for a child to lose parents at such a young age; even my schooling wasn't so great because I ended up getting bullied at school.

'Mike? You've gone silent again.'

'Sorry, Noeleen. I was just thinking about the way I got bullied at school because of my situation.'

'You mean because you were sad all the time?' she asks.

'Yes. It was horrible the way kids treated me. The thing is I lost all my friends because moving to the orphanage meant a change of schools. The kids weren't so nice at the new school …far from nice. I used to get a nice packed lunch and a bottle of water, and the other kids would take it from me; it was always the same guys. They would wait for me near the gates and raid my bag as soon as I got to school. It was an endless cycle of torture. I used to tell the nuns about it, but they didn't care at all.'

We should sit down and relax for a while, as she wants to get to know me a bit.

'Shall we sit down?' I ask.

'Yes, okay. You show me where.'

I slide my fingers through the gaps in her fingers, and we walk to the end of the enclosed area; the huge rock formations tower us in every direction. I sit close to the water flowing down the wall but far enough away that I wouldn't get wet. She sits down beside me and rests her head on my shoulder. She grabs my arms and wraps them around her – so sweet. I pull her hair and rest it on her shoulder so it's not in my face and hold her tightly. The ground here is nice to sit on; the thick grass is comfortable.

We don't bother moving the backpack; it's still in our line of vision, and Lido is still near it. Lido insists on scratching at the backpack; I can't understand why.

'Why don't we stay in this world forever, Mike?'

Is she being serious? Not even if you paid me would I want to stay, but I keep that to myself. She doesn't know what she's saying. This world is too weird for my liking. There's no day and night; it just randomly goes dark. And the creatures here aren't to be trusted. Plus, where would we start? We can't live in a cave all our lives. Bad idea, Noeleen, bad idea indeed. 'Naaaah. Let's get out of here, shall we?' I say in a humorous way.

'Continue your story then. You're not going to get out of it that easy, Mr.'

Oh god, she wants to hear more of my shabby life. For an instant, I thought she'd forgotten. Guess not. Well, what if she doesn't like me when she hears the rest? I need to keep back some information, as I don't want to put her off. It's not like she has deep feelings for me and she will stick around no matter what. What can I tell her?

'So I never went to college. Didn't care to, to be honest. I needed to get out of the orphanage, and I worked in a small clothes shop earning minimum wage. That was good enough. And at age eighteen, I had enough money to find a room. I lived in a shared house with some other housemates. We all had locks on our doors and didn't interact much. I kept to myself inside most of the time when I was off work. Shall we get moving?'

'Yeah, sure,' she agrees. 'I really enjoyed your story. I hope you can tell me more.'

'Yes, there's lots more to tell. But we do need to move from here. Let's see why Lido is scratching at the bag. That is really annoying me now, and I'm very curious.'

CHAPTER 25

The Mysterious Egg

I get up from my sitting position, helping Noeleen up in the meantime. I kiss her on the cheek and whistle at Lido to call the creature over. He doesn't respond at all. In fact, he is starting to get quite aggressive with the backpack.

I move close and kneel down, unclipping the clips on the backpack and opening it. Looking inside, I notice the shell of the egg is cracked slightly.

'Look here. This is why Lido is scratching,' I explain.

'Ah, Mike, the egg is hatching. How exciting,' she says.

I grab the egg carefully, remove it from the bag, and place it on the soft ground. Lido instantly goes to it and starts bashing the egg with its snout. Must be a way for the egg to hatch. I don't interrupt at this stage, as I can't be sure what will happen. Lido seems to be crashing at the egg with some force. Slowly, the crack on the shell is getting larger and larger, until a small piece of the eggshell falls to the ground. Some white light escapes the egg, suggesting that inside was nicely lit.

I pick up the eggshell to examine it. From the inside, it seems to be quite smooth, suggesting that this is a mechanism to stop the creature inside the egg from getting hurt during development. The outside is like delicate porcelain, and the nice colouration on the egg has completely disappeared. It's a dull shade of white now. The rest of the egg had also become white. Perhaps this is because the light has escaped from the egg, changing the colouration at the same time.

The thickness is no joke. This isn't something you can crack easily. It's about three times as thick as ceramic tile. No wonder Lido is finding it difficult to open the egg. I try to help out, but no matter how much force I put on it, the egg won't break for me. Lido seems to be doing a great job, as slowly, the hole is getting bigger and bigger, leaving crumbs and bits of broken shell on the ground.

I kneel on all fours and take a peep inside the egg. Nothing to see at the moment – just a lot of thick fluid. And I can see something else, presumably the creature moving inside. I can also hear tiny squeaking noises. On earth, baby crocodiles make noises to call their mums while they're hatching. The mum then helps the babies to the lake or river. Lido could be interested in the egg for two reasons – either because there's a tasty morsel inside or because Lido is the mother of the creature inside that egg. But what about the rest of the eggs in the ocean that Lido had pointed out? Will they die or what? Maybe Lido didn't necessarily lay the eggs and creatures like Lido take initiative and care for each other's young. This is where my curiosity bugs me. I would love to find out more about these creatures. As much as I would love to get out and get back to reality, I am actually enjoying the exploration part of this adventure.

As there's nothing to do, Noeleen and I wait patiently for Lido to finish his thing. Still, I can't wait for whatever is inside that egg to be revealed. I'm very excited. Lido seems knackered from trying to crack open the eggshell fully. I wish I could help, but the shell is too thick, and we have no tools to open it with.

We are safe as we hang out in this valley; nothing's here but huge rock formations on either side. It's a huge space here and quite tranquil. The water at the end of this dead end runs underground, and I definitely don't want to go back down there.

After quite a bit of time, Lido lies helplessly on the ground, apparently exhausted from all the bashing. The egg is open, and looking inside it, I see a little creature moving in a thick liquid.

I sit beside Lido and pull him onto my lap, stroking his head. He purrs and shuts his eyelids as I stroke his head.

'Oh, poor Lido,' Noeleen says.

'Come give him some attention.'

She gets up from her sitting position and sits beside me. She starts tickling the creature's neck and stroking her hand across his body.

'Let's take him home with us,' she whispers in my ear.

I actually wish we could. He's the perfect pet I think. 'I wish, sweetheart.'

She looks at me and frowns, as if she was a little girl and I just told her she'd have to give up her favourite My Little Pony. The thing is, I want to keep him as much as she does, but I know this isn't real. No way can this world or the creatures on it be real. It's too good to be true. And besides, imagine taking Lido out for walks. People would be screaming, as he doesn't exactly look like a harmless dog. On the contrary, he looks aggressive. And that would bring a lot of attention my way, which I wouldn't be able to handle.

Prrrrrrr. Prrrrrr.

Slowly Lido seems to be regaining his health. His tail whips me in the back as he excitedly responds to being stroked by me and Noeleen.

'Ouch!' I shout.

'What's up, Mike?'

Laughing to myself, I answer, 'I'm being whipped in the back by his tail.'

'Oh, man up,' she replies.

'Hold him on your lap for a while and see if his tail hurts you. I think she is a female, you know.'

'How can you tell?' she asks.

'Well, look at the way she or he was bashing the egg. At first I thought she would eat the creature inside the egg, but now that the egg has cracked, Lido hasn't attacked it. She left it there. We can't be sure of her, or his, gender yet.'

'We'll have to wait and see what the little fellow does, eh,' she says.

'Yes, give it time. We'll soon know if our friend here is going to take care of the newborn or just leaves it there. But if Lido leaves it there, that will just open up new questions. The most important question of all – why?'

'Give it some time, Mike. I'm sure you'll figure it out.'

Yes I will. I need to know why Lido was opening the egg. And why did the egg contain light inside? That's just strange. Where did that light come from? Ahhhh. So many questions and so few answers. Would be great to discover something new here. But at least scientists have equipment to run tests and such; all I have is a simple brain and clues about what's going on.

I place Lido on the ground again, to see what he actually does. Slowly, Lido crawls towards the egg. He's still tired I think and possibly hurt from the bashing. He wraps his body and tail around the egg, presumably protecting it and shuts his eyelids. He has also changed the colouration of his crest; it's the same colour as when I got attacked. Lido must be protecting the egg, which makes me think that Lido is a female. Usually males don't protect their young in the wild, with an exception for some newts, for example.

'How sweet. Lido's protecting the egg.'

'Yes, Noeleen. She must be female, right?'

'You never know,' she says and shrugs.

So Lido is having a nap, and Noeleen and I are here in this valley having to wait for the creature. I pull Noeleen towards me. She falls on my lap sideways.

'Miiike. You could have just told me to come closer to you.'

Mmmm. She winks and smiles at me. Moving to my front, she sits on my lap facing me. She leans forward and starts kissing my neck.

'Mmm, you are so beautiful and so sexy,' I whisper.

I can hear her breathing heavily as she presses her lips and tongue against my bare neck, occasionally sucking my earlobes. I grasp her hair with my left hand, and my right hand massages her sexy backside. We kiss passionately as things get heated up.

'I'm so wet for you,' she says, breathing hard.

I wink at her. 'You want me deep inside you?'

'I want it all inside me, deep, and I want you to do me hard.'

She starts kissing me again uncontrollably, lifting herself off me and unbuckling my belt and then pulling it off. Now she's unbuttoning my trousers, sliding her hand down my boxer shorts and taking a handful of my genitals. She's so reserved but naughty deep down.

I unzip her dress from the back and slide it off her. I rub her hard. I can feel how wet she is.

We play with each other, which eventually leads to us making sweet love on the turquoise grass.

Lido starts waking, making noises and looking over Noeleen's shoulder. He yawns widely. She rides me hard and grinds her hips, moaning with intense pleasure. Both my hands grope her breasts, and I play with her nipples.

I'm breathing very hard as she moans and rides me. 'Lido is waking, babe.'

'Ignore It. I want to give you pleasure.'

I grab hold of both her arms and hold them tightly behind her back. I make love to her like nothing else matters. Hearing her say my name gets me more aroused and makes my senses go crazy.

'Ahhh, Mike, you're so good.'

'Mmm, Noeleen, I never want this moment to end.'

Hot sweat drips off my forehead as I exert myself to please her every need.

'Harder,' she moans.

'You like this, gorgeous?'

'Mmmmm. Don't stop, Michael,' she says.

Both our minds are going crazy, and we are oblivious to anything around us. By the time we're finished, our sweaty bodies lie on the grass. We are totally exhausted.

'Let's get dressed, babe,' I whisper in her ear.

I pass her the dress and slide it over her head. I pull it down for her and zip it from the back. She stands up and arranges herself, brushing her messed-up hair with her fingers. I pull my boxers and trousers up, tighten the belt, and pull her down towards me so she's sitting on my lap again facing me.

I give her a peck on the cheek and hold her close.

'That was amazing, Mike,' she whispers in my ear.

'Want to do it again? Round two?'

'I would love to, but Lido is awake. And we should get back to reality. I can't wait for round two though.' She giggles and wraps her arms round me.

We cuddle for a few minutes. I close my eyes and nod off, but I keep waking every few seconds, realising I can't sleep.

'We better get up and start moving,' I say.

'Yes, you're right. I'm falling asleep, and we can't exactly sleep comfortably here.'

She gets up. I immediately follow. I grab the backpack and pull the straps over my shoulders. Lido stretches out and picks up the larvae from the egg. He holds it in his mouth and seems to be chewing on it.

'Mike, Lido's eating the baby.'

'No, no. I don't think so. Maybe he's cleaning it,' I suggest.

It could be that Lido is eating the newborn, but I don't think that's the case, given he spent so much time trying to get the egg open and didn't dive right in. Lido couldn't have been that hungry. I walk towards Lido and kneel down to examine the situation. He opens his mouth wide, and inside, it seems the baby has just been cleaned up. It's quite safe and seems to be in no danger. The eggshell lies on the ground empty – all smashed up in tiny pieces. So maybe Lido is a mother or a female specimen in the end.

Lido gently drops the baby on the ground and nudges it towards my feet – suggesting she wants me to hold it. How sweet. I grab the little snake-like creature and hold it in the palm of my hand. The little baby creature moves slightly, feeling the warmth of my hand. There isn't much to it. It's a dirty pink colour with spots all over its body and has a slimy texture. Its eyelids are still closed. I open its mouth with my fingers; it has no teeth and no tongue yet. But I see a dark purple colour on the bottom and top of the mouth.

Noeleen points beyond the valley's rocks 'Hey, Michael, look up there. Is that smoke?'

I look beyond the valley opening, and to my left, what looks like a bit of smoke rises. It isn't that far away, but I figure the source must be in an open area. 'Hmmm, that's strange. That definitely wasn't there before! Shall we get out of here and go check it out?' I say.

'Yes, sounds like a plan.'

She walks towards me and pokes the little baby creature in my hand. 'What are we calling it?' she asks.

'Did not know we'd be calling it a name. You can call it something, not too cheesy though.'

She giggles. 'Okay, I will.'

CHAPTER 26

Dead or Am I?

I place the creature near Lido and grab Noeleen's hand. We walk stealthily out of the opening in the valley, just in case there are some aggressive creatures around here. The path we came from is visible but far away, as we had been walking for quite some time. In front of us, rows of trees that seem to have been planted in the rocks bear yellow leaves. It doesn't make sense as usual, but what can I say. Crawling close to the trees are these crab-like creatures. They're not the usual crabs with the claws but more like antennae. They seem harmless and aren't bothered by our presence.

The smoke seems to be coming from behind the trees to the left of the valley we were in. This means we'll be moving further away from the path. We can't get lost here, as the path we came from is always more or less much visible. And even if we did get lost, we could always just walk around. Eventually we would find a familiar place.

'Hold on to me!' I say.

'Okay. This bit is scary! What are those things crawling around on the floor?'

'Don't worry. I'm here. Try not to step on them as we move through the orchard area!'

She's afraid I think, but she knows I'll protect her from anything. Lido follows willingly. I don't even have to call her over. She carries the baby creature in her mouth and doesn't seem as active as usual.

Just then, Lido notices the little creatures crawling around. She lays the baby creature near my foot and darts off towards them, picking them up one by one and swallowing them whole.

Noeleen giggles. 'That's funny. Lido must be very hungry. She is devouring them all,' she says.

'Yes, I suppose she would be hungry; she hasn't eaten anything for a while now.'

'Neither have we. I'm actually quite hungry, Mike.'

'So am I now that I think about it. We can actually eat the leaves here– well, not these yellow ones but the ones from those other trees with the pod-like fruit on them,' I tell her.

Her interest turns to the yellow trees. 'Have you come across any of these yellow trees?'

Thinking about it, I realise this is the first time I've seen them. And now, she'll probably make me try one of the leaves. She's too predictable. What if they are poisonous, though? Ahhh, I can't be sure.

'Would you like me to try one?' I ask, smiling big at her.

'Was going to ask you, if you could do that actually.'

I knew it. She wouldn't try them herself. She's too afraid. I walk over to the nearest tree, which is very close to where Lido is massacring those crustacean creatures. As the tree is quite low and the leaves are at my reach, I grab hold of a few. I hesitate to nibble at one.

'Come on, Mike. You can do it!' she shouts.

Eventually, I take a nibble at one. I spit it out, coughing vigorously and holding my neck, as it feels like I'm being chocked. I drop onto my knees, signalling with one arm for Noeleen to come over to me. My breathing is slowing down, and my heartbeat seems to be racing. I feel like I'm going to black out. I press my eyelids hard against my cheeks and grit my teeth, gasping for air as I struggle to breath.

'*Miiiiike!*'

She runs over and starts rubbing my back.

'Nooeee ...leeeene, heeeeeelp.'

'Hang in there. Please don't die. I'm not going to leave your side,' she sobs.

I drop to the floor, spit pouring out of my mouth. She gets on her knees, and I can see her crying. I lie on the floor with my arm on the ground, holding the leaves in my hand. My body twitches, as if I'm having tremors. I open my mouth wide to take in large gulps of air. With one hand across my throat, I turn over to my side and face myself down. Facing the ground, I place both arms on the ground and push myself back onto my knees. I struggle – and fall forward onto Noeleen. She holds me tightly in her arms, assuring me she is near and here for me no matter what.

She sobs. 'Why did I make you eat them? Why couldn't I keep my mouth shut? I'm so sorry, Mike. I don't know what to do. Please forgive me.'

I poke my tongue out at her and smile. 'Forgiven.'

I cannot believe she fell for the joke. What a good actor I am. She starts hitting me, as if I'd cheated on her or pretended to be dead. I laugh hard.

'You made me worry so much! Don't ever do that again, Mike!'

Wow she has really taken the joke badly. I still don't feel sorry, as it was a good joke and she should appreciate my acting skills. Yes, it was childish, but what man isn't? No matter how old we get, we all stay childish in some ways, after all.

'Hey, don't be mad! I'd thought you'd find this funny!'

'Funny?' she retorts, still yelling at the top of her voice. 'This is not funny, Mike. What if you were like that for real?'

'Okay, please don't shout.' I grab hold of her and hold her tightly. 'Don't be mad at me, baby. I didn't mean to scare you. It was just a silly joke. The leaves taste good, by the way – a little bit like lemon and a slight pineapple aftertaste.'

I get up to stand and help her up. I pull down some leaves and offer one to her so she can have a taste. She grabs one, and like me, she hesitates.

'Go on,' I say.

I push her hand gently, gesturing for her to eat it.

She takes a small nibble from one.

'Mmmmmmmmmmmmmmmmmmmmmmmmmmmmmmmmmmmmm mmmmmmmmmmm.' She must like them, as she shoves the whole leaf in her mouth. I do the same. I haven't really felt hungry since eating those boiled eggs. I'm not sure how to explain that. I'm not sure how to explain anything.

We both keep eating these yellow leaves. They have a smooth texture and a nice crunch. Examining one closely, I notice the pattern on each leaf is the same – symmetrical thin white lines form the leave's skeleton. Nothing in this world is ugly. Even the bark of this tree isn't brown but a dark maroon. As I did with the other trees, I scratch the bark with my key. The key goes straight through the bark, which seems to be made out of some kind of sponge – a very moist sponge. I cut a piece of the wet spongy bark of the tree and squeeze it hard. Liquid drips from it as I squeeze. I lick the wet end of my finger to taste this liquid.

'Yum.'

'What is it?' Noeleen immediately asks.

'This liquid coming from the bark tastes amazing – like something I've never tasted before; it's sweet.'

I hand over the sponge so she can have a little taste. Maybe she can identify what it tastes like. 'Taste it. You will definitely love it, and hopefully, you'll recognise the taste straightaway.'

She doesn't hesitate but squeezes the sponge into her palm and tastes the liquid.

'Oh god, Mike, this is good,' she says.

At least she liked it. I wonder if the sponge is edible. Taking it back from her, I take a bite out of it.

'Yuck.'

I spit it straight out. Despite the deliciousness of the liquid, the sponge itself made me heave a little. It was disgusting, horrendous actually, and even made my eyes water. And the texture gave me chills down my spine. I spit out as much as I can, while Noeleen rubs my back.

'There you go, babe,' she says.

She hands me a handful of leaves. I eat to relieve my mouth from the disgusting taste. As I slowly chew the leaf, my taste buds are coming back to life again.

'Better?' she asks.

'Yes. Thank you so much, sweetheart.'

I pull her towards me and give her a hug and kiss on the cheek.

'Shall we stay here and eat some leaves for a while? Lido is still gulping those creatures down, so we might as well eat, eh. We may not get many chances,' I add.

'Sure, I'll get some more.'

I smile at her and continue nibbling at the couple of leaves she gave me. They taste great. I wonder about these leave's nutritional value. They taste quite sweet, so their sugar content must be high – perfect vegetarian food. I'm not vegetarian myself. And neither is Noeleen.

It's bliss being out here, and the smell of the trees is very soothing to my senses. The sun is still huge and high up in the sky. One of the moons seems very close to this place. It's huge. I can even make out a forest on it. I wonder where that came from. I didn't really notice it there before – unless it's one of the other moons, and as it spins around this planet, it gets close and then goes far away as it circles on the other side. Jupiter has a moon like that. Life – the universe, the sun, and us – is amazing. I think of the way our bodies work like machines, perfectly timed, to keep us living.

I wonder what Noeleen is thinking – maybe about nails or her hair being all screwed up and messy. I'm not saying anything about that. I don't want to get her paranoid. To be fair, for what we've done here, her hair is quite nice still, just a little bit messy.

'Hey, Noeleen?'

She's daydreaming I think, staring at Lido having his fill. Those creatures are plentiful; Lido must have devoured about 200 already. He must have a hell of digestive system to be able to digest all that shell. I realise I've not seen Lido excrete, not even once. Who knows what happens to the food once it's eaten?

'Uh, Noeleen.'

She doesn't answer me, as if she didn't hear me. Or maybe I'm on mute. I take a few paces forward and stand behind her, wrapping both my arms around her neck and kissing her on the cheek. 'Pssst, what you doing?' I whisper in her ear.

She jitters a little bit, as if I frightened her. 'Oh, sorry, Mike. I was thinking,' she says.

'Can you tell me about your thoughts?'

'Maybe later,' she answers.

Hmmm. She doesn't seem happy. I'll leave her to it for a while and let her come to me. She does give me a smile of reassurance, and that keeps me happy anyway. I stand near the bark of the tree, taking down leaves one at a time and eating them. They seem to be very addictive, like they contain some kind of drug or caffeine; I can't stop eating. *Must be the sugar content*, I conclude. This is like a natural high.

Lido seems to be relaxed now. I think he's a she, so I will say she from now on. She lies down on the grass. With her belly engorged from all the crab-like creatures she ate, she looks pregnant. But she's just bloated. I'm amazed at how many of the creatures she ate.

'Lidooooooo,' I call.

She slowly drags herself near me and nudges her head against my leg. The baby is left on the ground nearby and doesn't seem to be in danger. I kneel down and stroke Lido's head. The purring sound she makes is too cute, and this keeps me stroking her for a while. We can't exactly leave without Lido, so we might as well have our fill while we're here. We can always keep moving whenever. No rush at all.

I look over beyond the trees. The smoke still rises, and I wonder what's there. I'm both curious and anxious. For our protection, I'd better let Lido rest so she'll get her strength back.

CHAPTER 27

The Way Forward

Lido doesn't take long to get back on her feet. She seems to be getting her energy back as she digests the crustacean creatures, and her belly seems to be shrinking back to normal quite rapidly. If only humans didn't take so long to digest food. We wouldn't be so bloated for such a long time – especially after eating so much for so long.

Lido's running around and wagging her tail at Noeleen, suggesting she's ready to start moving again. She picks up the baby creature in her mouth and comes towards me.

'Noeleen, it's time to head out,' I say. 'We need to investigate that smoke over there.'

'Sounds good,' she says.

She comes close to me, kisses me on the lips, and then slides her fingers through mine, and we walk so we're behind the trees. The source of the smoke doesn't seem far away, and the ground is hard rock and easy to walk on. In front of us, hundreds of these trees stretch out, all in a line – as if someone planted them years ago. The rock under our feet is smooth, with the odd pebble here and there. I examine the bases of the trees as we walk. I don't see any cracks in the ground or imperfections. No weeds grow anywhere, and other than Lido's meal, I don't spot any wildlife.

As we walk, Lido runs ahead and then back to us. We take it slow and don't rush. Now and again, we hear a crunch sound as we step on the creatures crawling here – that crunch you hear when you step on a bug but louder.

'Ah, Mike, I keep stepping on these creatures. It's disgusting.'

Oh no, she's whining. I start laughing. 'Don't worry. They seem harmless. I quite like the noise they make when squashed.'

'It's not funny at all,' she snaps. 'They are creeping me right out.'

'Relax. I'm here, and Lido doesn't seem threatened, so we should be okay.'

I squeeze her hand to give her a sense of security.

We keep looking beyond the trees at the smoke, which is getting closer. Still, all we can see in front of us are rows of these magnificent trees and not much else. The rock we stand on seems to be of different colours in some of the areas, suggesting that it's not the same material. The soil underneath this rock must be rich, I surmise. This area reminds me of an orchard – although an orchard is usually in a field and, here, all the trees are planted in rock rather than soil.

Pointing into the distance, we see a nice aerial display. Some birds are flying in a synchronized motion.

'How nice is that,' she points out.

'I know, what a beautiful aerial display, eh?'

'Yeah. They just don't have a care in the world, and they seem so placid up there.'

She's definitely right about that. There must be hundreds of them flying around. I hope they aren't aggressive towards us.

I see what looks like an opening in the trees ahead, probably not more than forty trees away. We keep watching the display while we walk.

'What are you going to do about the window in your bedroom when you get back?' she asks.

'Well, first thing's first; I need to contact the landlord. Will send him a letter and will also send a letter to the council to complain about the state of the house. Then I'll have to take it from there,' I answer.

Talking about this winds me up a little, as I have complained several times and the landlord seems to ignore me. I haven't sent him a letter yet, though, so I'll do that ASAP – as soon as I get out of here. This place has definitely shown me perspective of my life.

'Pssst.'

'Yes, babe?'

She looks at me as if she wants to say something important. 'Are you going to miss this place when we get back to real life?'

Good question – I haven't really thought about it. I'll miss Lido for sure, and I'll definitely miss the edible tree leaves. Who wouldn't miss Lido though? What an amazing creature. And the richness of this place – full of all sorts of beautiful and priceless locations. Who needs a house when you have that cave? As much as I don't want to live in a cave all my life, I actually wouldn't mind. But hell no. I want to get back to reality now. 'Only Lido will be missed if she can't come with us,' I tell her.

'You know she won't come with us. Her kind of creature doesn't exist back home, eh.'

'I know. It's quite gutting, to be honest. But, hey, we'll have to get over it and move on.' I'm going to be absolutely devastated when we leave here.

But I know it's for good and that my life will get better if I make that little bit of effort.

As we get closer to the edge of the tree line, it seems we've come to a dead end. It's not a full-on drop, but we're standing on a cliff. I look below to assess the situation. I gaze into the distance. The smoke is coming from a log cabin not too far from here, but we need to figure out how to get down. I'm not sure what to do at this point. We could climb down, but I doubt Noeleen will be happy about that. Instead, I decide to start moving along the cliff and the tree line. It seems the cliff is on a decline; maybe it meets the bottom of the area.

'Noeleen, I think we have to move along the cliff. We need to get down there somehow.'

She seems okay with that, but she looks like she needs to rest. I decide that we shouldn't rest until we get to the log cabin, where I hope we'll find someone to greet us. I'm very curious at this point, and we need to find our way down this cliff.

'As long as there is no climbing involved, I'm happy.'

'Don't worry. I wouldn't want you to get hurt.'

It would be faster if we actually climbed down, but there is no way she'll be able to make it, and I'm not sure if Lido can climb. We start walking along the cliff's edge, looking around us as we go. To our right are those rows of trees, and to our left, the undiscovered world, waiting to be trampled on by me, Noeleen, and Lido. Whatever is out there looks beautiful and full of activity.

Slowly but surely, we should get to the bottom. The walk doesn't seem tiring, as we're heading downhill. Noeleen still complains as we walk, and she is tiring me out.

'Please stop, moaning, sweetheart,' I say.

'I can't help it. My feet are hurting from walking on those rocks.'

'Surely they can't be that bad. We haven't walked that much. And besides, we've been resting a lot.'

'I know. I'm sorry. I just want to get to that cabin so maybe I can put my feet up,' she says.

Lido is as lively as ever, jumping and running all over the place. She zigzags past each tree we pass, just like a little child. Her newborn protected from danger in her mouth. This must be a fun world for her. I wish I had her energy. The temperature seems slightly warmer than that in the valley area and more humid; my hands feel slightly sticky.

I walk along the Cliffside, and Noeleen walks along the tree line holding my hand. I don't want to risk her falling; she definitely would be hurt badly. We're still walking on rock, but as we descend, the surface is starting to change to the turquoise grass, which is quite a relief, as it's much softer to walk on.

'We are nearly at the bottom, lovely.'

'Ermmm. Is it safe down there?' she asks.

'Why do you ask that?'

'Well have a look for yourself. All I see is big animals in the distance,' she explains.

I take a closer look at the area to my left, and she's right in a way. We can't be sure if the animals there are aggressive or not. What she's pointing to looks like a heard of some kind of grass-eating mammals. I wouldn't think they're aggressive at all, though they may be territorial. That's why we'll have to be very quiet and stealthy when we walk through the area. We'll definitely have to stick close to the cliff base and walk alongside it till we get closer to the cabin.

In the distance near the herding animals, I see a large lake with lots of different types of birds bathing in it and what's seems like two large animals drinking at the edge of the lake. I don't see any predators preying on the herd. But maybe they're hidden somewhere.

'Looks like herds and different kinds of birds. Have you forgotten what we have with us?' I say.

'Are you talking about Lido?'

'Of course. Her venom is very potent, and no creature could withstand her bite. Plus we're on Lido's good side, and she'll protect us and the young creature she carries in her mouth. I dare those animals to try to attack.'

I wouldn't mind seeing Lido kick their asses actually. And the display she'd put up to scare away any animals that threatened us would be amazing. That beautiful crest all fired up and colourful. And that venom is enough to put a dinosaur down, let alone one of those animals we see in the distance. Still, I wouldn't want to be chased by that herd. I can't see them well, but they look hard as rock and very well armoured. I might have to get a closer look at them when we get down there.

'What would you think if I said I wanted to go close to that herd over there?'

She shouts at me, 'Are you crazy?'

'Shushhhhh, don't shout. You don't want to get us unwanted attention. Maybe I am a little bit crazy, but I think it would be worth it to see those animals up close. Don't worry. I won't put you in any danger. I know what I am doing.'

I smile at her and think, *What have I gotten myself into!?* Might be a suicide mission going near them. But this is the only opportunity I have, so I might as well take advantage of the situation. Noeleen doesn't have to come, but she should; it would be a new experience for her. For me, it will definitely be an exciting experience; once again, I wish I had a camera on me. I didn't see one in the backpack, which is a shame. I'll have to write about these new animals in that notebook.

'Do what you want, Mike. But you are not leaving me alone. Plus, I don't want you to get hurt. Why would you put yourself in danger? What is your problem? I wouldn't go near them. What if they kill you? What if I end up alone in this world? Have you thought about that? You are putting me off going down there now. We should head back. I'm sorry!'

Wowww! Where did that come from? She is panicking badly, and she wants to go back. She pulls my arm as she tries to walk away.

'Mike, let's go back please. I'm scared.'

'Relax, sweetheart. Don't worry. Nothing bad is going to happen to us. I promise. When have I let you down before?' I forcefully pull her close to me, stroking the back of her head with my left hand and holding her tight with my right. I can't let her go back. We need to concentrate on finding our way out of here. She needs to relax. I'll do whatever I can to calm her down and keep her from going insane. She really flipped out. She must have been holding that anger and fear for a while and keeping it to herself. Now that I think about it, she was acting strange earlier and not talking much. Just gazing at Lido and thinking, she said. She must have been thinking about the situation we are in and panicking. She's probably freaked out by everything around us, including Lido. I am finding all these new things very interesting and couldn't ask for anything else; I have everything right now – Noeleen, Lido, and I'm still alive so far. Great friends are the most important part of life.

Slowly, Noeleen seems to be coming back to her sweet self. Her breathing has slowed back down, and her heart isn't thumping like it was previously. I could actually feel her heart beating hard when I first grabbed her and held her in my arms.

'I'm so sorry, Mike,' she whispers.

'Why are you sorry?'

'Because I got really scared and panicked.'

I pull away from our hug and place my left hand on her cheek and my right hand on the back of her neck. I gently press down on the top of her spine and massage her – a great technique to calm someone down. 'Oh, don't worry about that. It's normal to get scared, isn't it? Everyone gets scared now and again, even me. I have felt petrified while I've been here. I've been attacked twice before, and if it wasn't for Lido, I wouldn't be here with you. I am here for you, and I'll do whatever I can so you come out of this alive.' I kiss her on the forehead and smile at her.

She smiles back at me and hugs me hard. 'Thank you,' she says.

'Come on. Let's keep moving. We're nearly at the bottom of this cliff.'

The bottom is perfectly visible, and I can just feel the soft grass under my feet coming up.

'You know what?'

'What did you do, Mike?' She laughs as if I'm about to say something funny.

'I haven't had a cigarette craving since I've been here with you.'

'Really? I'm proud of you; maybe this is your time to quit.'

'Maybe. That might be the best idea that you've come up with today.'

'Wicked, glad I made a difference.'

Damn she is so beautiful. I just want to kiss her sexy body right here, right now. I can just imagine her riding me again, kissing me passionately, moaning and screaming my name as I make love to her.

As we walk down the cliff line, I take a sneaky look at her peachy ass. Damn, she is just perfect.

'Mike, what are you doing?'

Shit, she caught me. I start looking around and up at the sky, so maybe she won't notice what I was doing. 'Nothing? Was just …. Okay, I was looking at your sexy bum,' I say, stuttering.

'I knew it.'

Now she's looking at my ass. She laughs. 'Not too bad yourself, Mike.'

Her compliment makes me blush immediately.

At least she's relaxed and joking around with me again.

Only a few more trees to pass, and we'll be at the bottom at last. I take a quick glance behind and to my left. The smoke still rises from the log cabin, but now I can't see the cabin anymore, as there are trees around it blocking our view. We will get there eventually.

We make it to the bottom of the cliff and start moving along the base. I abandon the campaign to get close to the herd, as I don't want Noeleen to get scared or panic again. I hate seeing her like that, and it's not fair for me to put her in danger like that. I do feel a little bit sad that I can't go up close, but hey, that's that.

I look at the front of the cliff. What a good piece of architecture. The top is pure rock; a huge chunk of the top sediment is solid. Then underneath, I see what looks like some kind of soil, very green in colour with brown features. I touch the base; it's solid but crumbles slightly as I put force on it. I didn't pay much attention on the rock, but as we walk past the herd, I stare at them. They don't really do much – just graze and socialize with each other in their own ways.

'Mike. Let's go,' she blurts out.

'Eh?'

'Come on. Let's go near that herd. We have lido to protect us,' she explains.

Wow really? She wants to go near them? She must feel guilty, as she knows how much it means to me to go and explore the animals here. We have to move very carefully, and we can't look like a threat to them. Lido is just running around the field.

'Are you sure, sweetheart?' I ask.

'Yes of course. Let's go.'

'Okay, but we need to tread carefully. We can't talk at all, as they have probably never seen humans here before.'

My excitement heightens. I can't wait to get up close to this intriguing new specimen. But I'm nervous too, as we may need to run at some point. They're huge. And they could easily trample all over us and Lido. She is so tiny next to these animals. I still cannot believe Noeleen is willing to get close to them.

I signal with my hand to move forward. 'Okay, crouch and follow me.'

Very slowly, we move in our crouched down positions. Lido just runs ahead towards the creatures, but they don't seem bothered by her presence. They don't even flinch as Lido runs around their legs and even climbs onto their backs. They must be used to Lido's kind.

We get to around five metres away from one of the animals in the herd.

'Get down, Noeleen,' I whisper.

In front of me is a huge animal similar to a mammal back home. The bulky body reminds me of a rhino, but huge plates, each with a colourful design, cover its sides and back. The armour even covers its tail, which dangles and looks similar to a horse's tail except it has feathers on the end instead of hair. The feathers are blue and green, and the armour plates are dark brown, with purple and red patterns all over them. The creature's head is very oddly shaped, and some kind of bone protrudes from its head, slightly curved and going backwards. The animal's forehead is solid bone, but black hair covers both it and its eyes. As it grazes, the animal makes sounds similar to a buffalo's call, probably to communicate with the other members of the herd. Size wise, they're each about the size of a minibus. I wouldn't want to get trampled by one of them. There'd definitely be no surviving that.

'Mike,' she whispers.

'You want to go back to the cliff line?'

'Yes,' she answers.

'Okay, go. I'll follow you.'

She stands up and walks quickly back to the cliff's base. It's very sweet of her to allow me to examine these beasts closely, even though she's terrified, which is obvious in the way she nearly jogs back. I follow without hesitating. I look back, and Lido is still being Lido, jumping on the animals and frolicking. I would not want to be the newborn; stuck in Lido's mouth at the moment.

'Liiiiiido,' I shout.

'Miiiiike! What are you doing? Don't get their attention.'

Shouting like that was not a good idea. The animal nearest us pulls its head up and faces me, as if it might charge.

'Should we run?' she asks.

'No, don't run. Just stand still and let's see what happens next.'

Lido gets down and stands in front of the animal, displaying her crest, likely as a deterrent to keep the huge beast from attacking us. The mammal-like animal instantly backs down and resumes its normal grazing position.

'Phew.' Noeleen sighs with relief as the animal backs down.

Lido runs towards us, wagging her tail. I crouch down, stroking her head. I can't exactly thank her, as she won't understand, but petting her seems like a great idea.

CHAPTER 28

The Woods

We resume our movement towards the log cabin, still walking along the cliff base. I now and again look towards the smoke, as that's our guide to finding our way there. It's not that far at all now. Only a good ten-minute walk and then we'll have to walk through the woodland. The trees are very tall there, and if it wasn't for the smoke, we wouldn't be able to see the log cabin. The trees look like forest trees, each growing as tall as they can to reach as much sunlight as possible. Deep in the woodlands, it will be quite dark, with only random rays of sunlight filtered through the trees.

I take initiative and tell Noeleen we'll need to run to the other side. We'll have to cross this open field, and we can't draw too much attention to ourselves. It would only take one bite from a venomous species of bird, and we could be dead.

'I'm going to run towards the woods. Make sure you follow, sweetheart,' I say.

'Don't worry, Mike. I will be right behind you. I definitely can't get lost. Can I hold your hand while we run? I will feel much safer like that.'

'But of course. And don't worry; nothing is going to happen to you while I am by your side. You have my word.' I assure her.

'Thank you, Mike.'

I start running, holding her hand. I just hope nothing attacks us. The soft grass beneath my feet makes the run very comfortable, and the woodlands get nearer and nearer.

The trees tower over everything, and the smoke has now disappeared, as we are at the woodland's entrance. We just have to be sure to keep walking straight; if we get lost in these woods, it may not be so easy to find our way out of here.

'Mike, why don't you mark every tree we go past with your key?' Noeleen suggests.

I grab her face with both hands and squeeze her cheeks. What an idea. I didn't expect her to come up with that. 'Noeleen, you amaze me. Well done; what a plan!'

I kiss her on the lips, and we get moving, my keys in my hands. There are a lot of trees, and they are very close together, so I won't mark every tree. Instead, I decide to make a mark on every other tree we pass. And as long as we keep moving forward, we should get to the cabin alive and not get lost.

We move to the second tree in our path. I start scratching the bark with my tree.

Frustrated, I comment, 'Hey, this isn't working!'

No matter how hard I scratch, nothing happens. The bark seems scratchproof, but surely, that's impossible. I give it another shot. This time I move onto the third tree. I scratch as hard as I can. 'Ahhh, what are these trees made of?' I ask myself as I scratch.

'Let's just move on, Mike. They can't be scratched. We have to just try and not get lost. Simple,' she proclaims.

It's not as simple as she says. Think of how many people get lost in forests on earth. Without a compass, there is a possibility we might get lost here.

'Let's just see what happens. We have to come out of the place eventually. We could walk on the outskirts of the woodlands, but then that would be risky. Or we'll just have to say screw it and move through the woodlands. Your choice.'

It's better I let her decide, so she doesn't complain about whatever I decide; that should avoid an argument.

'Tough choice, eh. Let me think. Hmmmmmm. Let's go through the woodlands,' she says.

'Okay, let's go.'

We start our little adventure through the woodlands. My suit is still slightly damp from swimming, but it's not unbearable. We go past a lot of trees, hundreds of them, all towering over us. It seems as though they've been here for thousands of years, with each tree more than 100 metres tall and not much growth on the ground. Even the grass is a greyish colour, compared to the turquoise grass everywhere else – which makes a lot of sense, given that the sunlight undoubtedly gives the grass its beautiful turquoise colour and not much sunlight reaches the forest floor.

Now and again, we pass a few spots where sunlight reaches the ground, but not much light exists here. The woodland is dim compared to the rest of the world. And it's somewhat scary. Now and again, we hear animals, presumably calling each other. This has both Noeleen and I on edge, and Lido seems to have her guard up. She's protecting the baby creature, as well as us.

Clutched onto me and clearly scared, Noeleen says, 'This place creeps me out.'

I pull her close to me and put my arm around her, which keeps her from freaking out at every little noise we hear.

'I'm so scared.'

'Don't be, sweetheart.'

There seems to be something, or rather some things, watching us from high up in the trees. I can't make out what they are, but they seem to live in peace, as they don't bother us. They keep jumping from tree to tree as we pass. I get the binoculars out of the backpack and try to take a closer look at them.

I can't see much, but they seem to have more than four limbs and are no bigger than a football. They can't be insects – unless they're giant insects. They don't have much colour on them, which makes them hard to see, as they're nicely camouflaged, presumably for protection.

The best thing we can do is to ignore them, as we don't want them coming down here. It seems like there are loads of them jumping from tree to tree. On the ground itself, nothing seems to be a threat, with the odd insect here and there.

'Are those things dangerous, Mike?'

'I'm not sure, to be honest. Let's hope not! Lido seems to be in defence mode and sticking quite close to us.'

'Do you think she can sense danger?'

I really don't know. I'm only guessing, but I have to try to keep her calm at all costs. Otherwise, we'll lose our bearing and end up getting lost in this woodland.

'I think she's just protecting her young,' I reply.

'Oh, yes, I forgot that she has a baby in her mouth.'

'We'll be okay, sweetheart. You worry too much. Think about how protective Lido would get if we got attacked, considering she has a baby in her mouth,' I point out.

'Yes, true. She would go absolutely mental, eh.'

We come across a big area where some sunlight has come through and is hitting the ground. Where the sun's rays hit the earth, some type of plant is sprouting. I go close and examine the little plants. They look like small tree sprouts. Their leaves, seven per stem and all facing the sunlight, are blood red, and the plants seems quite sturdy. I realise they're growing the same way plants grow back home.

It doesn't seem that we've walked much, but we've actually covered a lot of distance, as the edge of the woodlands is now out of view.

'We have walked loads since we've been here, haven't we?' she says.

'Yes we have; good old exercise.'

'Definitely good exercise. I think I've lost some weight, but I still look fat.'

Oh no, not this crap. Why would she say that? Her body is amazing. She thinks she's fat, but I call it slightly curvy.

I laugh and push her gently. 'No way. You are not fat at all. How can you say that about yourself?'

She shrugs and avoids the question; deep down she knows she is gorgeous and that her figure is far from fat. But she may be slightly insecure. She did mention how her ex used to bring her down constantly.

I don't understand women sometimes. They have hundreds of guys chasing them, and then they bring themselves down. It sounds like fishing for compliments when they talk like that. But on this occasion, I do think Noeleen is being genuine. There are plenty of reasons not to argue with a woman. And this would be one of them.

'Is that the end of the woodland, Mike?'

'I can't be sure yet. I don't think it'll be long before we get there. Let's just hope we're not far from the cabin once we're out of this place.'

'Yeah, I agree with you,' she says.

It doesn't take us long before we reach the outskirts of the woodland. And we're still safe and sound. Those creatures jumping from tree to tree have stopped bothering us, and now we stand at the edge of this dark woodland.

'You see. I told you that we would be fine.' I say, relieved that we're still okay. 'You should learn to trust me a bit more.'

'I know, and I'm so sorry for the way I am. My ex changed me. I never used to be like this before I met him.'

'He really played you, didn't he?'

'Yeah, he did. Really badly. He didn't care at all about me. He just cared about himself and no one else,' she explains.

'I'm sorry, sweetheart.' I give her a hug to reassure her that things are different now that she's with me. 'Cheer up. Look over there – the cabin. And is that what I think it is?'

'Wow. At last we're here. And what are you pointing at?' she asks, all confused.

'Surely you can see exactly what I'm seeing.'

CHAPTER 29

Father?

Up ahead lies a nice peaceful open area, and in the middle stands the cabin – a small wooden dwelling. Sunshine rains upon it. Sitting on a rocking chair, looking relaxed, is what seems to be a guy reading a book.

'Noeleen, tell me you see that guy.'

'Yes I do. He looks quite relaxed on his rocking chair. Where did he come from, do you think?'

'Well he must have been here for a long time now, as he has a cabin. He must have built it, unless it was already there in the first place,' I say.

'I'm done with trying to understand, Mike. Let's go say hello, shall we?'

'Yes, let's do it.'

We cautiously walk over to the gent sitting on the rocking chair.

'Lido, get back here. Come here, girl!' I whistle as Lido runs ahead.

Lido sure seems curious. She goes to the guy on the rocking chair and nudges him to stroke her. He doesn't hesitate and doesn't seem afraid of Lido at all. In fact, he stands up and starts stroking her head and crest. Lido spits out the baby from her mouth near the guy's foot – as if she wants him to see her baby.

'Hey, Noeleen. He hasn't noticed us yet. Let's see what he does. Crouch down.'

We both crouch near the edge of the woodland, curious as to what or who he is. From this distance, I can't tell his age, but he doesn't seem that old. He walks towards the door and goes inside, shutting it behind him.

'I wonder what he's doing.'

Looks like he went inside his cabin. I don't actually say this out loud, as it would sound way too sarcastic. 'Let's wait here and see what happens. We can't be too sure at the moment.'

'You're right.'

Of course I'm right. What if he is a danger to us? Well wouldn`t Lido sense that If he was? I keep asking myself stupid questions all the time. Of course, Lido would protect us. She's always been there.

Noeleen tugs on my shirt as the man comes out of the front door. 'He's coming out,' she whispers.

'Yes,' I whisper back. 'I can see that you know.' I laugh quietly, as she seems to be getting way too excited about this guy.

'What are you laughing at?'

'You, sweetheart.'

'Why?' she asks.

'Well, the way you where tugging on my shirt as if I couldn't see the guy.'

She giggles and nods at me. The guy has come out with some kind of fish clutched in his hands. He places it on the ground – a great way to get on Lido's good side. He seems to know what Lido likes, as she instantly starts taking chunks out of the fish carcass and swallowing them whole.

The man sits back down on the rocking chair holding the baby creature in the palms of his hands.

'Let's slowly move and introduce ourselves. Maybe he knows a way out of here,' I say.

'Yes, okay,' she agrees.

We stand up and start moving towards the man. It doesn't take him long to notice us.

'Hey, over here!' he shouts.

Wow, his voice sounds familiar. I lift my arm up to acknowledge him. As we move closer, it seems I know this man. But are my eyes deceiving me? Is that who I think it is?

'Noeleen …'

'Yes?'

'Noeleen … Oh my god—'

'Mike what?'

'That guy. It's my …my …'

'Who is it?'

'I can't believe it. It's my dad. What is he doing here?'

'Is it? Well, don't just stand there. Run over to him and say something.'

'You're right.'

I instantly run over to the man.

'Daaaaaaaaaaaaaaaaaaaaaaaaaaaaaaaaaaaaaaaaaaaaaaaaaaaaaaaaaaaaadd
dddddddddddddd!'

'Son?'

He stands up and opens his arms. I hug him, crying my eyes out. 'I thought I'd never get to see you again.'

'You were so small when I last saw you, and look at you now, son. I've been watching over you since we parted. You need to move on with your life, Michael. You have a great future ahead of you if you just believe in yourself. You haven't had it easy like other kids, but it`s not too late,' he says.

'Why did you leave me, Dad?'

'I never left you, son. I've always been watching over you.'

'Where's Mum?'

'Your mum is in a better place' He looks straight into my eyes. `I was stuck in this world because I am constantly on your mind, my boy.'

'But Mum has been on my mind too.'

'I know, I know. Who's your friend?'

'Yes. I'm so sorry I didn't introduce her to you.

'Noeleen, come here.'

She walks over looking all shy and grabs my arm.

'Noeleen, this is Dad. Dad, this is Noeleen.'

'Pleased to meet you, Dad. Mike told me all about what happened.' She smiles and giggles as she calls him Dad.

'Call me John.' He puts his hand out to shake her hand. They seem to take a liking to each other.

Dad sits back down on his rocking chair.

'How did you guys end up here?' he asks.

We look at each other and shrug our shoulders. And if Dad got here after he died, does this mean we died also? Okay, things are starting to make sense. I only went out for a few drinks the other night. Did anything else happen, and I can't recall? But I wouldn't have gone out in my work suit.

'Erm … Not sure on my behalf. What about you, Noeleen?'

'I have no idea. I just woke up here,' she says.

Dad stands up.

'How do you like my little cabin then? I built it all by myself,' he says.

This is impressive work. The cabin's all made of wood, and it has a porch on the front and enough space for a rocking chair. Four steps take you up to the front porch area. The wood itself is very clean cut and seems like it has been painted, but I don't think he painted it. 'Wow, Dad, this is true craftsmanship, good quality work. How did you manage without tools?'

'I found lots of tools when I first got here. And I even have electricity inside,' he explains.

'How did you manage that?'

'Let's just say this world is truly magical. Everything is possible.'

It seems so. Noeleen seems be baffled by all this. I can imagine she's also amazed by this work.

'Why don't you two come inside?' Dad says.

'Come on, Noeleen.'

Dad places the baby creature near Lido and opens his front door. The door itself has been professionally carved, and the pattern on it is really intense. He signals for us to go in first.

The first thing I notice is the sheer size of the hallway. As you walk in, a mat on the floor bids 'Welcome.' A beautiful light beige carpet covers the hall, and there is a marble sculpted archway as we walk through the first part of the hallway.

Noeleen pulls me over to her and whispers, 'Wow, Mike.'

'I know right? How can this be? The cabin looks small from outside, yet the interior looks huge.'

Dad talks with his head held high and proud. 'Told you that, in this world, nothing is what it seems.'

He has been here for over twenty years, and I'm sure he's seen it all. And how he has managed to build this place from scratch is beyond belief. Magical, indeed.

Dad points out the rooms. 'First door on the left is a small bathroom. Second door on the right is the cinema room.'

Did he just say cinema room? I don't believe it. But I'm sure my beliefs will be thrown out of the window when he actually takes us to the room.

'Cinema, Dad?'

'Yes of course. Your old man needs entertainment.'

He hasn't changed one bit. He's still the man I remember – full of life and a sense of humour like no other.

'So straight on there is the kitchen, which is an open plan with the dining room. Then beyond that are the back yard and the yacht. Haven't taken it out for a while, so maybe you and Noeleen will join me at some point?'

'A yacht? Impossible. The cabin is surrounded by woodlands. There's no sea here,' I say.

'Mike, Mike, Mike, you will have to see it for yourself then.'

This guy is nuts. How did he build a yacht here? I look at Noeleen, and she seems as dazzled as I feel. A yacht? He must be pulling our leg. What's upstairs … a helicopter? And I really hope he doesn't say he has a helicopter. That would be ludicrous. 'Yeah. I believe you, Father. Don't worry.' Well not completely, but I have to believe him, as he'll have to take us for a yacht ride round the place.

We follow him into the cinema room. Both Noeleen and I are completely gobsmacked and cannot believe our eyes. This room is absolutely gorgeous. Red velvet embroidered cloth covers the ceiling, and the walls are all a dark grey, with spotlights neatly placed inside the wall. The seats – around fifteen of them set out in rows of three – are all top quality sofas. Each row is higher than the one in front of it, just like a proper cinema. The screen itself is around ninety inches wide.

'I'm not even going to ask where you got these from,' I say.

'John, wow, I love your style.'

'Thank you, Noeleen. Make yourself at home. I have every movie you can think of, if you want to watch something later.'

She giggles, as she does, and nods.

'Why don't we head to the kitchen and make some food?'

'Well, we ate some leaves from some trees earlier. Are you hungry, Noeleen?'

'Yes, I am a little peckish and curious about what food exists here. What's on the menu, John?'

He takes us into the kitchen, which is situated at the end of the hallway. The furniture is very contemporary, with burgundy red cupboard doors and drawers and a breakfast bar with stools around it. We take a seat, while Dad rustles up some food. The dining area looks more like a living room, with a nice flat-screen TV and a cream leather L-shaped sofa. The walls are all painted magnolia, and the floor is solid oak. Beautiful décor. Dad definitely has style.

The back door is a patio slide door with blinds to block the sunlight from coming through.

It doesn't take Dad long to cook, and it seems like we're being served some kind of bird he probably caught from this place.

'Try 'em out,' he says.

Noeleen and I look at each other.

'You first,' she says.

'Not a problem. They smell tasty.'

I sink my teeth into what seems like a leg. The meat is very tender and falls off the bone with no problem. 'Yummy. Wow, this is good, Dad. Tuck in, Noeleen.'

She takes a small bite and chews on it for a while. 'Mmmm. Mike, this tastes amazing; your dad is an amazing chef.'

'Well, thank you,' he says. 'I'm going to show you your bedroom as soon as you finish, as it will get dark soon. Then tomorrow, we'll go on my toy, or what I prefer to call her, *JJ Boat.*'

'Interesting, Dad. I'm not even going to ask how you have managed to get this stuff and the boat. I do need to ask what it is with the night-time situation here.'

'Yes, Mike, good question. Night-time doesn't happen often, but I've gotten used to the signs that indicate when night-time will commence.'

I finish off my food and sit here feeling slightly bloated, confused, and not sure what is happening. My dad has appeared from nowhere, and I'm left with more and more questions. Does this mean Noeleen and I are dead? I certainly don't remember dying. And if I'm dead, why am I thinking and feeling everything that is around me? Why do I have feelings for Noeleen? We can't be dead. I only went out for a few drinks that night before I woke up and ended up in this place. Regardless of the fact my dad is here, I still need to get back to the real world.

I wish I could take my dad back with me. It's sad that I might have to part from him.

'Come on then. Let me show you the rest of the house and your sleeping quarters,' dad says.

'Yes, okay, let's go.'

We all walk to the hallway, and Dad leads us up the staircase. The stairs are carpeted in a thick white carpet, and the banister is beautifully carved and made of wood. Unlike my stairs, these do not creak at all as we go up.

On the wall, I see pictures of the flying creatures swarming the island Noeleen and I saw. The photographs are beautiful and show the creatures' magnificence.

When we get to the top of the stairs, Dad explains, 'So here in front of us is the bathroom.'

He opens the door, and inside are what looks like a Victorian sink and toilet with a stand-alone Jacuzzi bath in the middle of the room. The taps look like gold, and the shower rests on the handles on the bath.

'Those are solid gold, my son – worth a fortune down on earth.'

'Wow, no way. They look beautiful. The bathroom looks great,' I say.

On the wall, a thirty-two-inch TV gives the room the finishing touch. And a thick bath matt covers the floor. Egyptian towels hang from a golden towel rack. This is pure luxury.

'Wow, John, this bathroom is the most gorgeous bathroom I have ever seen.'

'Thanks, love.'

We exit the bathroom and turn to a door to the right, presumably leading to a bedroom. There's another door down the hallway.

CHAPTER 30

What a Beautiful Home

Dad points over to our sleeping quarters. 'Over there is your bedroom,' he says, pointing to the far door, 'and this one is mine.' He points at the door closest to us and then walks us over to our room. He pulls down on the handle and nudges the door open. 'Hope you have a comfortable sleep here.'

'Dad, wow, are you serious? How did you manage all this?'

'Don't question or complain, son. This is the luxury you and your lady deserve for the night.'

I look at Noeleen, and she's wearing a smile of excitement, as if she has just been taken to the Maldives for a holiday. The room is huge, the bed is queen sized, and the sheets seem to be made of silk. A small bedside cabinet stands on either side of the bed with a small lamp on each one. In front of the bed attached to the wall is a fifty-five-inch screen and, to its right, a cabinet filled with collectable dolls. To its left, another cabinet is filled with model planes.

The carpet is a cream colour, and the wall behind the bed is a glossy maroon. The other three walls are all a nice light coffee colour in matte.

On the other side of the bed, I notice what seem to be two doors. 'What do those doors lead to, Dad?'

'Why don't you go and find out for yourself? I'm going to go and get tucked in. If you need anything, come knock on my door,' he says.

Before he leaves, he gives me a hug. 'Good to see you again, son.'

'Yes, Dad. I love you.'

'Love you too, my boy. Never forget that.'

He leaves us in the room, shutting the door behind him.

'Mike, your dad is a sweetheart, and this house is overwhelming. I wonder what's behind those two doors,' Noeleen says.

'Well, we will soon find out for sure. You take the door to the right, and I'll take the one on the left?'

'Yes, sounds like a plan, Mike.'

We walk over to the doors. I stand in front of the one on the left, and Noeleen stands in front of the door to the right.

'Okay, open on three. One …. Two …. Three ….'

We open the doors at the same time and walk into the rooms.

'Ahhhhhhhhhhhhhhhhhhhh, Mike.'

'Are you okay?' I ask.

'Yes, this room is amazing.'

'This one's an en suite bathroom with what seems to be a shower/steam room combination. There are even places to sit, and the room and the smell in here is ravishing,' I say. 'What's in that room?'

'Come here and check it out,' she says.

I walk out of the en suite and over to Noeleen. I cannot believe my eyes. I'm looking at a huge aquarium built inside two of the walls, housing fish I've never seen before and the most beautiful plants I've ever set my eyes upon.

The gravel looks like gemstones and diamonds, sparkling as the light from the tube goes through them. A nice cream L-shaped sofa rests against one wall, and at the end of the sofa is a small table. To the right of the door is a fridge full of soft drinks and deserts.

'Is that chocolate?' I say.

'Yuck. I don't like chocolate; it's disgusting.'

Who doesn't like chocolate? How weird is that. 'Never thought I would hear anyone say that, you know.'

'Everyone has things they don't like,' she says.

I grab her hand and take her to the sofa, lie down, and pull her down on me to cuddle up. The room décor is very peaceful, and so is the sofa itself. It's way too perfect. So comfortable.

She lays her head on my chest and relaxes. The pump in the aquarium makes a nice bubbling sound; the water ripples, and effects reflect onto the ceiling as a vibrant display.

'I'm so relaxed, Mike.'

'So am I. I don't think we'll be using the bed tonight.'

I gaze at the ceiling as Noeleen rests her head on my chest. The reflection of the water makes me feel drowsy, and I'll nod off soon. Noeleen hasn't taken long to fall asleep. Her eyes are shut, and she's breathing steadily, resting one of her legs over mine.

I'm so sleepy, I'm shutting my eyes.

'Goodnight, sweet Noeleen. I love you.'

She's sound asleep and doesn't say anything back. I shut my eyes and doze off.

CHAPTER 31

The Yacht

Loud knocks at the bedroom door wake me up. Noeleen sleeps soundly.

I slowly get up, rubbing dried mucous from my eyes. I get off the sofa slowly so Noeleen will stay asleep and go out into the hallway to greet my dad.

'Morning, son. Wakey wakey.'

'Morning, Dad.' I say, yawning widely

'Come down with me. Let's make breakfast together. Noeleen still asleep?'

'Yes, she is.'

'Father, son time then.'

Dad leads the way to the kitchen, and I mostly watch as he prepares breakfast, as I'm not sure how to cook stuff in this world. It's all new, including an array of different meats, to me. He pan fries most of the strange food items, while I watch him show off his cooking skills.

'So, Mike, did you learn anything from your old man when you were a kid?'

'I got your sense of humour, I suppose. I was put in an orphanage, and a kid taught me how to shave and stuff like that.'

'I'm sorry you had to go through that, my boy.'

'Not your fault, Dad. You were driving sensibly as usual.'

'Yes, but you can't dwell on these things. You need to move on, son. Remember what I always used to say. Never dwell on the bad but try and change it all into good.' He pauses as he flips over the meat in the pan. 'Always remember that, Mike.'

'Note taken, Father. How long until breakfast is cooked? Shall I go get Noeleen?'

'Yes, sure. Go wake her up for breakfast. It'll be cooked in around four minutes,' he says with a grin.

I get off my stool and make my way up to the bedroom.

I can hear her singing in the en suite.

'Noeleeen?'

Nothing. She must be taking a shower. I try to walk into the en suite to let her know that breakfast is ready, but the door is locked so I go back downstairs.

'Hey, son. Noeleen still asleep?'

'No, I think she's having a shower.'

'You should have joined her.' He winks at me and smiles.

I instantly blush, as I get shy. I never expected him to come out with that. I refrain from saying anything and just nod.

'Did you at least tell her breakfast is nearly ready?'

'No actually, I didn't do anything. The en suite door was shut, so I didn't bother her.'

'Get yourself upstairs and tell her that breakfast is nearly ready.'

'No problem, Dad.'

I run back upstairs and go straight into the bedroom. I knock on the en suite door and shout out, 'Noeeleeeen, breakfast is nearly ready!'

'Wait there,' she calls back, 'I'm just putting my bra on.'

A couple of minutes go by, and she comes out of the bathroom in her underwear. I turn my face as I get all shy around her.

'Mike, you don't have to be shy. You have seen me naked before. Could you pass me my dress please? It's on the bed.'

I walk over to the bed and grab her dress. I help her get dressed by sliding it over her head and pulling the zipper up from the back.

'Let me brush you down a bit. The dress is slightly dusty,' I offer.

'Oh, thank you,' she says.

I brush her down and pick small pieces of fluff from the dress.

'Nice and tidy now. Come on. Let's not keep my dad waiting,' I say.

Downstairs in the kitchen, we sit on the stools before a nice plate full of colourful food, as I'm calling it, and the cutlery.

'Try that juice. I made it from those yellow-leaved trees,' Dad explains.

I grab my glass and take a sip out of it. 'This is great. Shame it doesn't exist back home. Try it out, Noeleen. Tastes like the leaves we ate.'

She doesn't hesitate and tries it. 'This is very refreshing, John. Thank you so much. And the breakfast looks delicious.'

Dad sits down opposite us, and we all start eating breakfast. Dad reminisces about the period of my childhood he was alive for, embarrassing me in front of Noeleen in the process. We also talk about our journey on *Boat JJ*.

'Dad, I miss Mum so much.'

'Me too, son. That day was not our day.'

'I just wish I could tell her that I love her and see her again.'

Noeleen rubs my back, as she can tell I am getting sad about this.

'There, there, Mike. She is always by your side. She knows we love her so much. Come on. Eat your breakfast. We have a trip on my yacht to look forward to.'

He's right. I have to be strong. I pick up my cutlery and start eating. The plate contains all sorts of food items, and dad's cooking does taste absolutely gorgeous. I haven't had a breakfast like this in years.

It doesn't take us long to finish eating.

'I'm going to go and start getting ready. I need to get out of this suit and have a shower.'

'Okay, me too,' Dad says.

Upstairs, we both get ready to go out. The suit is a bit too scruffy now, but it's all I have. Dad's stature is much larger than mine, and his clothes wouldn't fit me.

The water pressure in the shower is just perfect, and the temperature is soothing to my skin. I don't spend much time in there though, and within no time at all, I'm back in my scruffy unkempt suit.

I go downstairs, and Noeleen isn't in the kitchen. I step outside the front door, and she is there playing with Lido.

'Hey, I'm ready, sweetheart.'

'Hey, Mike. Is Lido coming with us?' she asks.

'Yes, we should take her for a ride. She'll love it.'

'Let's get going. Is your dad ready?'

'Not sure to be honest. But we can wait in the kitchen.'

She grabs Lido in her arms, and we walk into the house. Dad waits in the kitchen area dressed in a white shirt and beige trousers. But he's wearing flip-flops, which makes him look slightly odd.

He shouts across the hall, 'Come on, son. Let's get going.'

We walk over to the double sliding doors in the back of the kitchen. Dad slides the door, revealing the back garden.

With amazement, Noeleen says, 'Michael, I want this garden.'

I smile. 'I wouldn't mind that either, you know.'

The elegant setting of this garden is alluring. The smell of the fresh cut turquoise grass is an essence I've never smelled before. On the left-hand side of the garden, a hedge trimmed in the form of a roaring lion stands tall. And on the right-hand side is a row of stunning plants, all different colours.

Flat stones placed on the turf lead to the yacht, which is parked in a calm purple ocean, just on the other side of the garden.

Noeleen and I look at each other in amazement.

Dad, who's by the yacht, signals us to join him. We make our way along the flat stones and arrive near the boat parked nicely in the slip. The decking seems to be made of solid wood, nailed down and held together by rusted nails. The wood itself is veneered, which gives it a nice finish. And on the edge of the slip, a sturdy wooden fence with an opening to the ramp leads to the boat.

We walk up onto the deck. The stunning workmanship on the boat's foredeck is spectacular. A beautifully polished golden rail stretches around the entire yacht. The boat itself is no more than fifteen metres long and is all in a white gloss finish. A distinct red painted line circles around the middle of the boat, and *JJ Boat* is painted on its front. On the aft deck, a large raised deck salon with a U-shaped settee enables a panoramic view. Before the entrance to the galley is a nicely shaped solid gold rail, and three steps made of the same wood as the cabin lead down.

'Let me give you a tour of the boat. Follow me.' Dad goes down the three steps into what he says is the galley. This is where he does all the cooking. It's furnished with a small sofa and table and, on either side of the cooker, a couple of granite worktops. The cupboards all look like they're made of solid oak. Even the smell of the oak; smells quite good.

'All the food is kept in those cupboards over there,' Dad says. 'Please help yourselves.'

At the end of the pathway inside lies one of the bedrooms. It's a tight fit, as it contains a double bed quilted with a nice grey silk sheet.

Dad gestures forward. 'Straight ahead lies the yacht's master bedroom. We have two more bedrooms and a little bathroom. Come have a look at the switchboard.'

We walk over to the switchboard, which is located over Dad's bed.

He points out the different switches as he explains, 'These two switches need to be on at all times. This red switch needs to be switched on if you wish to take a shower. And then this switch here,' he adds, pointing to a huge blue button protected by a plastic casing, 'this one we only use in emergencies.'

It looks very tempting to press, but at this time, I restrain my curiosity, as I don't want to anger my dad. I'm sure it's important, and if I pressed it something we'd regret might happen.

'Take me away from here, Dad. I'm curious now. I want to know what that button does.'

He gives me a disappointed look. 'Do not press this button, boy.'

'Yes, sir, I won't. Don't worry, Father.'

Noeleen just smiles and nods at everything dad says. She seems to be keeping a distance from me, but I'm not sure what's on her mind.

Lido relaxes on the foredeck.

Dad walks towards the aft deck. 'I'm going to start her up, and we can set off.'

I follow to help him and watch him as he prepares the boat to set off. He hauls up the anchor and detaches the ropes that keep the yacht parked. He then sits himself down in the cockpit, which is situated in the aft deck, behind the wheel.

As we set off, the calm purple ocean swell gently collides with the side of the yacht. The sea breeze sprays in my face as I look ahead. Seems like there is a coastline to the left of the boat. The sun shines high above. The sea shimmers as the sun's rays make contact with the water.

'Noeleen, you have to come out here.'

Nothing – she does not respond. I go inside the yacht, and she is just unwinding in the galley. Relaxed.

With my arms crossed I look at her. 'Are you okay?' I ask.

She looks at me and frowns. 'I'm fine. I don't feel like coming out. I'll stay here,' she responds.

I don't say anything but decide to ignore her somewhat chilly tone, walking over to Dad instead.

'Where are we heading, Father?'

'I'm taking you to an island not far from here. It's full of creatures you'll appreciate. We'll have to keep our distance, though, as they're hostile.'

My eyes widen, and with an immense smile I respond, 'Sounds like fun, Dad.'

I can't wait till we get there now. I forgot to bring the backpack, which is a shame. But I'm sure we'll be going in close enough to see the creatures without the binoculars.

CHAPTER 32

Beautiful Ocean

The boat swiftly floats over the ocean currents, revealing spectacular views. To the left of the boat, we pass the mountain range where the first cave was situated. Now I understand why the cave couldn't have possibly led to the other side of the mountain.

The huge rock pile, securely stuck together as if with glue, towers and is visible for miles. The tip of the mountain is covered in snow, and dark blue clouds blissfully sweep over and collide with the mountain, dispersing into smaller clouds.

'Beautiful sight, eh, Dad?'

'Yes, son. I do come out a lot in this, and sometimes I even fish in these areas.'

'Have you ever come across any storms around here?'

'Yes actually – twice. The lightning strikes hit the yacht's mast, and it snapped in half, nearly sinking my yacht. Luckily I got out of there alive and sailed back home. What's up with Noeleen? Why isn't she out here with you?'

I shrug my shoulders, confused. 'Not sure, Dad. Thing is, we get along so well and I treat her really well. Even the way things have panned out here suggest we're meant to be together. But the problem is she doesn't trust guys that much.'

Dad nods as he steers the boat with the waves. 'Your mother used to show cold remorse towards me at times. But that's how they are. You have to be patient. And don't smother her, or it won't end well.'

'Do you think about Mum much?'

'All the time, son, all the time. She's always there smiling at me. I tried to be near her, but god sent me to this world instead of her world.'

'Did you search for her?'

'Yes. I searched every inch of this place. The island isn't far from where we are now. We'll soon be close to the island's cliffs. I can't get too close, though. Got stuck once, as I wanted to explore and the boat got caught between two rocks.'

'At least you managed to get out.'

'Yes of course, or else I wouldn't be here, eh.'

'I wish we could have more conversations like this.' I bow my head in silence, a wave of sadness hitting me.

'Cheer up, son. Nothing we can do. Unfortunately, life is set out like that. We have to just move on and keep living. In my case—'

He stops talking. I think he doesn't want to upset me by pointing out the obvious fact that he's already dead. But I understand what he's trying to say. I am happy I have this opportunity to talk with him. Noeleen worries me a bit, as she hasn't set foot out of that galley. I do wonder what she's thinking and hope she's not having second thoughts about us after all we've been through. I'm used to women leaving me now. I don't understand why. I never cheat, and I always treat a woman I'm with like a princess.

Dad points at the base of the cliff as he steers the boat round to get a closer look.

'Is that what I think it is?'

'What do you think it is?

'Looks like a will-o'-the-wisp.'

The cliff base opens up into a cavern, and inside, a beautiful wisp hangs and swirls and drifts about in the open space. The light blue magic sparkles as it dances inside the cavern.

'I haven't had the chance to get close to it, but it's magical. It has always been here every time I've travelled to this area.'

'Dad, it's absolutely fascinating.'

I pop my head down into the galley in an attempt to talk to Noeleen. For some reason, she doesn't seem happy. She just sits there with her arms crossed, engrossed in her own thoughts.

'Noeleen, come check this out. It's magical.'

She doesn't say a single word to me. Dad said not to smother her, so I decide not to say anything else. I'll let her mope around and feel sorry for herself.

As Dad sails near the cliff, I take time to silently enjoy the view. The cliff base isn't supported by anything; on earth, it would surely collapse, as deep inside the cavern, the purple ocean crashes against the fragile rock, eating away its heart. The wisp seems to keep the cliff intact and stable, and as it clashes with the rock, it disappears and forms elsewhere inside the cavern. This magic creates the very soul of the cliff, magically flowing in the slight breeze that is present.

On the other side is the tiny island Noeleen and I viewed before. It's still full of those flying creatures, but from here, it's not very visible, as thick fog clouds our view of it.

Dad questions me again about Noeleen; he seems concerned. 'Why isn't Noeleen joining us?'

'I have no idea. She doesn't seem to want to interact with me at the moment. Maybe it was something I said. I'm really confused and not sure what has come over her.'

'Want me to go see her?'

'Noooooooooooooooo. Please, Dad. It's okay. I'll deal with it. Like you said, I'll leave her to it. I have no choice, eh. She is acting fairly strange though.'

I don't have time to stress out. Lido sits comfortably on the foredeck, enjoying the ocean breeze, I'm sure.

As we pass by the cliffs, I notice pointed fins protruding from the sea. I point them out. 'Do you know what they are, Father?'

He takes a look. 'They're very similar to dolphins, and they're master swimmers,' he explains.

One of the sea creatures leaps out of the water. It's not very large and grey in colour. On the side of its head is what look like shark gills, and it has a blowhole like dolphins and whales do, which probably enables the creature to breath both in and out of water, giving it time to catch their unsuspecting prey. The skin would definitely dry up on land; it looks thin and brittle. They also seem to be social animals, as they're in a large group. Their dorsal fins cut tiny lines in the water as they swim blissfully past the boat.

'This water paralyzed me,' I tell Dad. 'I was walking on the seabed and swallowed some of it.'

'Yes, that happened to me too. But I came around after a while. One of my wild adventures was deep beneath this boat. Some rare materials exist down there. Brace yourself. I'm going to make a sharp right turn towards the island, as we're getting to shallow water here.'

I hold onto the rail on the edge of the boat. He spins the wheel sharply to the right, making me lose my footing and slip. I still hold on tight to the rails, and this enables me to stand back up.

'This boat is pretty nifty, isn't it?' He looks over at me. 'Your father built this,' he boasts.

And he has the right to boast. This is a great vessel. 'Of course,' I reply.

We're now heading straight for the island, sailing against the wind and towards the foggy outskirts of the perilous little landmass. I figure he won't sail too close. The island is hardly visible as a result of the fog blanketing it.

'Son, I don't think you'll get to see anything; the fog is quite thick. We'll try and go as close as possible. I can assess better once we get to the foggy area. Might be just a small patch.'

'No problem, Dad. I'm just happy to be on this boat with you.'

We sail at a slow steady speed, edging towards the thick fog. The ride is smooth, and the weather is excellent here. The wind blows lightly. I can hear nothing but ocean at this point, as we drift through the thick moisture in the air.

'Don't be afraid, son. We're still quite far from the island. This boat is equipped with sensors that detect landmasses nearby.'

I'm glad my dad's expertise can guide us through this dangerous patch. 'Thank you,' I say.

I worry about Noeleen sitting in the galley alone, unaware of the beautiful landscape we've just sailed past. I can't figure out what her problem is.

Dad points ahead of us. 'Look over there, my son.'

The fog is clearing as we move forward. The islet is more visible now, and the view puts me in a deep trance. I can't seem to turn my head away from it.

CHAPTER 33

Lido

'Stop the boat, Father!'

'Don't you want to encircle the whole island?'

'I think we need to be aware of those flying creatures.'

I'm sure he's come across them before, but I think of Rick, who died because of those creatures. And I don't want to put Noeleen in danger.

'I have a secret weapon for those creatures. Don't you worry, Mike.'

Secret weapon? I bet it's some ridiculous rifle of some sort. Knowing him, it's probably a rocket launcher. He gets closer to the island and starts circling the boat round it.

As he's doing so, I can see a large rock mass protruding from the ocean. It looked small in the distance, but up close, it's a different story. The rock looks like limestone and quartz, and the island looks to be rich in some silver metal, as the sun reflects off its mirrored curves.

'Dad, have you ever tried to get on the island?'

'No way. It's way too difficult. You see all that metal in the rock?'

'Yes. What is that?'

'I managed to pick some of it, and it's really malleable – similar to lead but it's got a much better shine to it. Lead itself looks quite dull'

I wonder what I could make out of it.

'Son, get down into the galley!' Dad suddenly screams. I look up and see a flying creature swooping towards the boat. The creatures are masters of flight, and we're definitely in a pickle. Dad tries to steer away, but all for nothing. I lie down, my chest pressing against the deck, which allows me to stay low and still keep an eye on my dad. He gets a device out of his pocket, no bigger than a whistle, and blows into it.

The creature speeds down to attack my dad. 'Watch out, Dad!' I scream.

He lets himself fall to the ground, and the creature barely misses him. 'I'm okay, son. This device will deter it.' He blows through it again, and Lido hisses wildly, flashing her crest up at the beast.

'It's coming back, Dad.'

'Son, get yourself in the galley. Now.'

I can't listen to him, and I remain on the ground. The flying beast doesn't back down but hovers over us, looking down at us and waiting for the right moment to strike. Lido seems to be protecting its young from the likes of the creature.

'Dad, I can't leave. I don't want to leave. I will stick by you no matter what.'

The device isn't working; it seems to be useless against the wild beast. 'I'm going to have to try and get out of this area, son. There's no other way. It will keep attacking.'

Dad pushes himself up from the deck and steers the boat away from the island. He sets the throttle at full speed. As the boat moves away, the creature doesn't flee but strikes once again. This time, it ruptures the main sail and again tries to attack my father. After a near miss, the creature ascends back into the sky.

These animals are highly territorial, and they do not like our presence here. We slowly edge away from this perilous chunk of rock. Dad keeps his cool, and as far as I know, Noeleen has no idea what is going on. Lido defends her young on the front end of the boat, hissing ferociously. The flying creature doesn't pay much attention to Lido but focuses on me and my dad.

As if it wishes a death sentence on us both, it hovers above the boat, following our retreat. *But Dad is already dead*, I keep thinking. So what if the creature does attack him? Surely nothing would happen. Come to think about it, am I looking at a ghost? I dare not think about this further, as it will make me feel sentimental.

'Sooner or later, it will leave us be, son,' Dad says. 'Just stay down and let me deal with it.'

'Stay strong, Father, and we will both keep an eye on it.'

Not much time passes before the creature seems to be bored of diving continuously. Just like that, the torment is over, as it flies off into the distance.

'Is it gone?'

Father looks behind him. 'I think so. I can't see it anymore. We need to be alert, though, as we'll be passing through the thick fog again.'

At last the creature is out of sight, probably back guarding its territory, and we sail away.

'Son! Get down!'

I instantly drop to the ground, slamming my chest across the wooden deck. The creature must have circled round the boat at a distance and is attacking from the front. Lido yelps as the creature flies over us, shadowing the yacht. I look up to examine its majestic features.

I notice Lido. The creature's lethal claws pierce Lido's fragile skull. Lido's body helplessly dangles in the air, and the baby has no doubt been pierced through. '*Lidoooooooooooooooooooooooooooo!*'

As the creature flies past the boat, Lido in its clutches, blood drips onto the wooden deck, soaked into the grain and staining the floorboards.

'Father, the creature has taken Lido. What can we do?'

He abandons the wheel and comes over. He helps me up and gives me a hug to comfort me. This is sad. I can't believe how emotionally attached I got to this creature. I cry my eyes out on Dad's shoulder.

'Son, you have to let go. Lido gave up its life so you can survive. That creature loved you as much as you loved it.'

'I can't understand why it's left me.'

'Go sit down on the settee, son. I'll take you home.'

I go to the settee and sit down, holding my face in my palms and crying my eyes out. The journey back home seems short, and I spend it sobbing on my own. In fact, I don't notice anything around us. And at this point, Noeleen is at the back of my mind.

Dad comes over and places his hand on my back and rubs. 'We're back now. I'm going inside, and I think you and Noeleen need to talk. She's waiting for you on the slip.'

'Thanks, Father, and I'm sorry. I got really attached to Lido.'

'I know, my boy. You're human after all. You can't help but develop strong attachments to a pet, but don't dismiss Noeleen. Get up and go speak to her.'

Dad goes back into the house, and I go down the boat ramp. Noeleen stands waiting for me.

'Hey, we lost Lido.'

She doesn't seem happy. 'I know, Mike. I wasn't near you when it happened, but I heard the commotion.'

'Everything okay?'

'Yes, I'm fine. Come on. We need to start moving again.'

I think she's fed up with being in this world and just wants to get out of here. I don't argue and decide to get going with her.

'Before we go, we need to spend some more time with Dad.'

'Yeah, okay.'

We walk over the stepping stones and across the garden. The patio door isn't there anymore. It's now just an old tacky, wooden door.

'Noeleen, are my eyes deceiving me? The patio door isn't there. That's my back door that leads into my house.' I stand there speechless for a moment.' Oh, not this again.'

She dismisses me completely as if I said nothing. 'Come on, Mike. We need to go.'

She opens the back door and walks inside. I follow and cannot believe my eyes. The inside of the cabin has transformed. The rusty fridge sits there making a loud clanking sound. The sink is full of dirty dishes and stagnant water. Why does this world keep emphasizing my house so much? This place makes me feel sick to my stomach. It's disgusting.

'Noeleen, wait …'

She walks ahead of me through the grimy kitchen, down the hallway, and out the front door.

'Dad? Dad! Dad, where are you?'

I run upstairs and check every room. He isn't here anymore. 'Daaaad!' I call. 'Where are you?'

No one answers.

I go back downstairs and leave the house. From the outside, the house looks the same as before. It's still the shape of the cabin. The rocking chair is empty. Dad is nowhere to be seen.

My emotions are running wild. I'm losing everything.

'Noeleen!' I call at the top of my voice, hearing the desperation in my tone. 'Wait up, please. We need to look for my dad.'

She stands at the edge of the forest while I resume my search for my father. I go back inside and examine every inch of the house. He's nowhere to be found. I wonder what happened. That he didn't even say goodbye saddens me.

'Father!?'

Where has he gone? This world is really cryptic, and I'm feeling way too disheartened to deal with it. What do I do now? I can't just leave. What if he comes back? I can't leave Noeleen waiting all alone. She might leave.

I stand in the house, dazed. Nothing is what it seems here.

I can hear Noeleen calling me, impatience in her voice.

I leave the house and catch up with her. We walk through the woodland. I start questioning the way she's being with me. 'Are you mad at something I've done?'

'No.' She just shakes me off with a one-worded answer, leaving me baffled.

We get to the cliff base, and I decide to confront her. She is acting too mysteriously all of a sudden, and it's bothering me too much. I stand in front of her, place my hands on her arms, and say, 'Noeleen, we need to talk.'

'I have nothing I want to talk about, Mike. We need to move on.'

'But this is the problem. Why are you acting like this?'

She shrugs and forces her way forward. 'Forget about it, Mike. I'm okay.'

As we edge closer to the path, I can't help wondering why she is acting like this. She doesn't say a single word to me, as if I no longer exist. I nudge her arm. 'Noeleen, will you say something, please?'

She dismisses me and moves on. I decide to keep my mouth shut. I walk, contemplating Dad's disappearance and Lido's death and Noeleen's coldness towards me. I can't help but feel rather empty inside. The pain slices through my fragile heart.

She suddenly stops in the middle of the lane.

CHAPTER 34

Bleeding Heart

She looks at me as if she has something to say.

'Michael, I'm so sorry,' she says.

Oh, what is she on about? A sense of disappointment creeps through me, and I'm overwhelmed by this gut feeling that either something devastating has already happened or it's about to happen. I got a hint that something bad was coming ever since we got off that yacht.

'Sorry? For what, Noeleen?'

She pauses, still staring deep into my eyes. *Say something.* I feel nervous, and I'm quite afraid of the next sentence she's about to say. My hands tremble.

She starts looking at the ground and muttering. 'I just can't—. I'm sorry.'

What is she saying? 'Noeleen?'

'Mike, I have really enjoyed my time with you, and I really appreciate everything you've done for me – the way you look at me and the way you hold me. And the way your lips feel against mine is truly amazing. The way you care so much about me and the protection you've provided me while we've been stuck here—'

I'm frowning, as I know there must be a but at the end of her sentence. 'Go on.'

Her eyes are wide open, and her lips shutter. 'I'm not sure what to say.'

I grab her arm and pull her towards me. She shakes her arm to force me to let go and resists my advances.

'Are you okay, Noeleen?'

'Michael, why are you so good to me?'

'I guess I've never met a woman like you before, and I feel like it's meant to be that you're here with me.' I smile.

She doesn't smile back but stares at the ground.

'Can you please come out with it and tell me what's troubling you?' At this point, I'm being sympathetic and still showing her that I care.

She doesn't say anything. She's acting weird and suspicious and doesn't seem to be able to open up to me. Maybe it's something I said? She's really confusing me. As much as I want to stay calm, I feel frustrated. It's like I don't exist at the moment. Is she devastated about the death of Lido? I feel sad about that, but I'm not taking it out on her, and it has definitely not changed the way I feel about her.

'Say something, please.' I mean, what did I say or do that was bad enough to force her to be like this towards me?

'Nothing,' she mumbles to herself.

'Then why the silent treatment? You're making me feel very nervous.'

Nothing. Not even a word.

She stands there doing absolutely nothing and looks at the ground. A few seconds pass, she faces me and looks me in the eyes. 'I can't let this continue, Michael.'

'Let what continue?' I'm so confused, so sad. Is she being serious right now? We've been stuck in this world together for all this time, and she talks as if she doesn't know what she's saying.

She says nothing. She needs to explain soon. These games are starting to make me feel agitated. I don't want to get angry at her, not now. There is no need for anger. But she really needs to spit out whatever is on her mind. I need to relax.

'Noeleen, let's talk. Why not sit down on the path? You can't treat me as if I don't exist.'

'No. I don't feel like sitting,' she says in a cold tone.

'Then just spit out whatever you need to say and get it over with.'

'Michael, just stop,' she says in a loud irritated voice.

'Don't speak to me like that.' Shouting at me isn't going to work. I can shout back, but I refrain for a while.

'Just stop going on about the same things then. Stop repeating yourself.'

'I wouldn't have to repeat myself if you just spat out whatever you had to say.'

'Maybe I don't want to talk. Did you ever think about that, Michael?'

'Maybe? What is this maybe about? I've done nothing but stand by your side all this time. And this is how you treat me?'

'I said stop, Michael!'

She's raising her voice at me. I have no idea what her problem is. She's treating me like crap, and it's really getting on my nerves. I start to feel anger, as if I need to break something. I'm boiling inside.

I decide to sit on the path and let her do as she wishes. As much as I care about her, at this moment I couldn't give a toss. Maybe she should learn how to speak to people and get some respect. I still don't understand why she's doing this, but it's best I let things be and stay out of the way for a while to calm down, as I will just keep getting angrier and angrier and will definitely end up snapping at her. I don't want to escalate the situation.

What do women want? I think hard about this. They say they want a guy to treat them with respect, and they want a loving man in their lives – someone who listens and treats them well. I am having second thoughts about this. I've done nothing but be there for this girl. Yet I'm the one hurting right now.

She walks over and sits beside me. She grabs hold of my hand and looks at me. 'I'm so sorry, Michael, but I'm not ready for a relationship with anyone at the moment. I really like you, but I don't trust anyone and can't give my all to anyone. I thought about this on the yacht, and it pains me to have to say these words,' she explains.

'Okay, so you don't trust me?' I keep my feelings locked up but can't stop a teardrop from running down my face.

'I just don't trust guys, Mike. My last relationship really hurt me and stopped me from doing what I want to do in life. My ex used to hit me if I didn't do what he said or disagreed with him.' She seems to be holding back a good cry.

'I understand, but not every guy is like that. Surely you have realised this by now.' I need to be careful about what I say to her. I really don't want to sound desperate. 'I understand, but I wish you never acted as if you were so affectionate towards me.'

She smiles at me and blushes. 'I wasn't acting, Mike. I don't trust any guy.'

'Relax, Noeleen. I'm not rushing anything.' I stroke her arm as I'm saying this, and I give her a soft smile.

She leans over and whispers in my ear, 'I'm sorry I acted up.'

She's apologizing? I really am confused. I can't understand what is going on right now.

I pull her closer and kiss her.

'Forgiven.'

'Mike, I'm sorry I'm still feeling the same as I did before. I have to go.'

Her body starts to disappear. My arm goes through her body as if she was a ghost. I see her crying. Then it's as if she was never even there. She completely disappears.

'Noeleen? Where are you, babe? Please come back.'

I stretch my arm out, waving it about in the air where she was sitting.

'Noeleeeen! Noeleen?'

What has happened here? Why has this happened? Where is she? I ask questions that no one is here to answer. Am I in an illusion?

I have lost everything. Lido, Dad, and now Noeleen. I'm a grown man crying his heart out, with nobody here to witness it. My heart is shattered. My breathing is getting heavier. I'm absolutely devastated. I stand and walk slowly.

What now then? She's gone, and I'm still here. I feel really angry and disappointed that she just decided to change her feelings towards me. Nothing makes sense. I was being myself and very affectionate towards her. And she threw it all in my face.

I don't feel like moving from here. I sit back down and place my hands on my head, grabbing a handful of my hair. A deep sense of frustration and sheer pain swell up deep within my soul.

'Pull yourself together, Michael.'

I should get over it and just relax. What happened with Noeleen was just an illusion. She must not exist. It's just that she seemed so real and true. I've been in this type of situation before. This always happens to me. Why can't love be simple? Why can't mutual affection and trust be enough? Life is like that – you're up for a while, and then without notice, you're down in the dumps.

What now? I really need to get out of here. I'm sick of this place. I feel another teardrop run down my face. I stand up and wipe my sorrows with my sleeve.

Not sure what I'm doing, I start walking straight ahead. I don't really care where I'm heading. Nor can I be bothered to explain my thoughts.

I shout at the top of my voice, 'Get me out of here!'

That's not going to help me at all. I need to figure this puzzle out, and quickly. So I found a note telling me she was near, and then she found me. We fell for each other, we were close, and the way we kissed was amazing. Then she disappeared. How can I be happy when I don't have a clue what to do next?

I miss Lido. I should have saved her. I miss Dad. 'I need you, Father.'

I talk to myself. 'What's the problem, Mike?'

Ahhhhh, please let me get back to my crap life. What am I still doing here? This illusion seems rather pointless. I can't think straight. I'm going nuts at the moment. My head is all over the place, and I'm not sure what I'm doing.

I start crying, soaking my face with my tears. I can't help feeling like this. I really started to adore her. Why have you left my side, Noeleen? Why did you freak out? I treated you right, didn't I? What did I do that was so wrong? My heart bleeds for you. Come back, my sweet Noeleen. Why did you stab my heart with a rusted dagger? It hurts too much. As much as I'm a strong man, I do fall for the wrong women, and I get hurt every single time. They say heartbreak makes you stronger. Is that really true though? Every time, it feels the same for me. I refuse to put a wall in front of me. I refuse to not let anyone in. I'm not the kind of guy who will use anyone for my pleasures, and I tend to trust too much.

I better keep moving. I need to try to get over her.

I look ahead, and I'm on the path walking uphill towards where I started my journey. I notice the trees seem to be dying; one by one, the leaves smoulder as if they're on fire and ashes fall to the ground, leaving nothing but black bark and branches. And the turquoise of the grass is fading to a transparent dull colour. The ground is becoming translucent. What is happening? On the ground, beneath the dead trees, hundreds of those pod-like fruit lie open. I look at the sky. The sun seems farther away than it was before. And the moons have totally disappeared.

It feels like Noeleen has taken the life out of this world, as she has taken my heart – hammered it to pieces, crushed it with her bare hands. It was a selfish act that will not be forgotten.

I look behind me; nothing is what it seems anymore. Everything is completely dead. Even the mountain where the cave was is just a huge pile of rock, as if someone has crumbled it to pieces. The path behind me is changing as I go, slowly becoming a dirt path – a path that no one would want to walk on. The boulders to my side have sunk into the ground, as if in quicksand. I look around for any type of animal. Surprisingly, I see nothing – not even a single bird or insect.

'I wonder what's happening here,' I say out loud.

Giving up is my only option at this point. I get on my knees and look up to the sky.

'Let me get out of here!' I cry out in sheer agony to anyone who might be listening. 'If you can hear me, please let me out!'

I shout helplessly, as if someone can hear my words of remorse – my words of desperation and despair. I hold my hands open in front of my face and gaze upon them. My skin …it's changing. My fingertips are slowly disintegrating.

As the air blows through my fingertips, the skin is coming off, and the remnants are lost in the wind. The rest of my hand is turning black, as If I'm suffering from frostbite. The longer I stay here, the faster everything is breaking down. But then what will happen after I'm a complete goner? Maybe I won`t feel like such a worthless miserable looser anymore. This is my destiny and my life. This world is my reminder of a non-existent future.

I start moving upwards as the dirt path has caught up to me. I run until I reach the end of the path. Nothing is here. It's a dead end, and the area that was once a desert and then a tropical area has totally disappeared, my view of it blocked by a brick wall, towering well over me and extending for miles – as if half this world is closed off to me.

'Wake up, Michael.'

It's her voice. That was her voice. Where is it coming from? What is happening? Is she watching me? 'Noeleen?'

'Wake up, Michael'

I hit my head with frustration, as I believe I'm going totally insane. I can definitely hear her telling me to wake up. But I am awake. My eyes aren't deceiving me. I can see everything that's going on around me. She's not here. I'm imagining things.

I shout insanely at nothing. 'Leave me alone! You *left*. Now let me be!'

'Wake up.'

That voice in my mind – go away. Get the hell out of my head.

'Michael, wake up.'

'I am already awake. Stop talking,' I shout.

Her voice echoes through my mind as if she's next to me – smiling at me, or in this case, laughing at my worthless self. I'm confused. What's going on? Why is she playing with me like this? I thought she was such a lovely person.

Once again, I look at my hands. I can feel them, but they're black, and most of my fingers have decomposed into nothing.

'Wake up, Mike. Listen to my voice.'

I cover my ears and shout, 'No. No! You are not here. I cannot hear you. I'm just going mad!'

'Wake up!'

CHAPTER 35

Awake

Bzz, bzz, bzzzz, bzzzz.

The alarm wakes me with a sudden fright. I barely open my eyes to look at the alarm clock. Seeing it's not even 6.00 a.m. yet, I roll over onto my side, closing my heavy eyes. I can hardly move, as I'm pinned down by my thick quilt – very comfortable, all tucked in, warm.

I pull my arms out from under the quilt and gaze upon them. 'Am I back home?' My hands are totally intact. I sit upright and rest my back against the cold headboard. 'Where am I?'

Bzz, bzzz, bzzz, bzzz.

The alarm's still going off. The lack of sunlight makes my room dark. I grunt and yawn, stretch my muscles, and rub my crusty eyes. I bash the alarm button to silence it.

Wow what a dream! What was that about? What detail. And Noeleen. She's not in my bed cuddled up to me. And dad? I rub my eyes with disbelief, and sadness runs through me, as though I was back at the day I lost both my parents. That world was perfect up until the end, where it turned out to be a complete nightmare.

I still gaze at my hands in disbelief that I'm back home.

The cold shocks my body, and I shiver uncontrollably. I need to get the window fixed. I told the landlord to come check it out a few times. But he ignored me. I tried to shut it with a hammer the other day, but the wood is so old and swollen it wouldn't even budge. Not to mention the state of the floorboards beneath it. *Soggy* is the word. It's been raining hard lately.

Without a care about the cold, I decide to get up and go for a shower. I really can't be bothered to go to work. But I have no choice. This hangover isn't helping either. I slowly get out of bed and get myself washed. It doesn't take me long to get dressed for work. I open the top drawer of my bedside table and reach in for a fresh packet of cigarettes.

I go downstairs and sit down in the kitchen. In front of me is the empty fruit bowl and an ashtray half full of old cigarette butts. I empty it and sit back down, sliding a cigarette out of the fresh pack and lighting it up in the process. The taste and smell disgust me a little. And it's making me feel quite light-headed. I don't think I can manage a whole cigarette at this time in the morning. I grab some change and decide to go to the bakers to buy a sandwich for work.

'Morning, Michael,' says Charlotte down the bakers. She wears a huge smile on her face, and she seems happy. She must be looking at me thinking, *Wake up.*

'My usual please, Charlotte. Exact money on the side here for you. Thank you.'

I'm half asleep and don't feel talkative. I reach into my pocket for the money and put the coins on the side of the counter.

She winks at me. 'There you go, Mike, your usual. Enjoy it.'

I smile at her, thinking how great she looks today. 'See you soon, Charlotte.'

As soon as I get home, I place the sandwich in my briefcase and sit back down at the table. Once again, I contemplate the dream. I see Noeleen's face smiling her beautiful smile at me. I think about the time we made love and her sweet personality.

It seems she is still in my dreams. And thoughts about her run through me uncontrollably. 'Get over her, mate,' I say out loud. 'She doesn't exist.' I shake my head in frustration. These thoughts cannot last forever.

I can't dismiss the dream, though; it must have a meaning. First things first. I need to send a letter to the landlord. And if he doesn't mail me back, I need to complain to the council. That has to be the reason my dream was so filled with this place. Noeleen and I ended up here, and Dad's cabin transformed into this grotty place. And the notes on the fridge were telling me to get out.

I'm amazed at how I can remember this dream in so much detail – as if it was real. The heartbreak with Noeleen, Lido, and Dad is still at the surface right now. And I can't help thinking about it.

'I love you, Father. I love you, Mother. Thank you both for being there for me. I know you can hear my words.'

I am so sure they can hear me and that they look over me on a daily basis.

I need to get myself some plants to give the place a nicer look, and I need to talk to my manager at work. I need that promotion. I can't live like this anymore.

The dream has opened my eyes and has definitely given me a goal to better myself. Lido and Noeleen might have been symbols that there are people who love me in this world and that I shouldn't give up on pursuing my dreams.

I open my briefcase and take my watch out. The time is 8.10 a.m., and I should set off for work. The weather outside is clear, but it's blistering cold out there. I wrap myself up and head out. I walk slowly, rubbing my hands and blowing hot air into them. The street lights are still on, as it's still quite dark. And the road looks barren. The only place that is open is the bakers. All the other shops are shut.

As I walk, I notice a girl walking towards me on the same side of the pavement. I push myself slightly against the wall to give her space to walk past. As she walks past me, she stares deep into my eyes. She smiles and keeps walking. I continue to walk but look back, catching her in the act of looking back at me. She looks very familiar, and memories of my dream flood back to me. I whisper to myself, 'Noeleen?'

This girl looks exactly the same as the girl from my dreams. And that look she gave me stabs pain in my chest, as I still feel gutted over the dream. Once again, she pierces my heart with a dagger, leaving me speechless and shaky at the knees. I wonder where she's heading. I have never seen her in these parts before. And my god, she looks amazing, as she did in my dreams.

I must shout her name. I must talk to her. I don't feel cold anymore, and my palms are sweating. I'm reluctant and can't seem to make that one move. We stare at each other for a few seconds. She looks forward and continues to walk.

I need to do something quickly. She's walking away, and I'll never see her again. *Call her name, Mike. Just say it, man.*

This is no coincidence. She has walked past me for a reason, and if I miss out on this opportunity, I might recall this moment with anguish.

I stand still for a while, filled with incredulity, not believing my eyes. Speechless and not feeling too well, I continue to walk forward again. Disappointment and sheer frustration fill me; I didn't have the guts to talk to her. I'm going to regret this day.

To be continued...

Lightning Source UK Ltd.
Milton Keynes UK
UKOW02f0315210115

244798UK00001B/70/P